W9-BUB-311

BUG GIRL

GIRL

FURY ON THE DANCE FLOOR

Benjamin Harper
Sarah Hines Stephens

Illustrated by
Anoosha Syed

[Imprint]
MAKE YOUR MARK
NEW YORK

A part of Macmillan Publishing Group, LLC
175 Fifth Avenue, New York, NY 10010

BUG GIRL: FURY ON THE DANCE FLOOR. Text copyright © 2018 by Sarah Hines Stephens and Benjamin Harper. Illustrations copyright © 2018 by Imprint. All rights reserved. Printed in the United States of America by LSC Communications, Harrisonburg, Virginia.

Library of Congress Control Number: 2017957953

ISBN 978-1-250-10663-6 (hardcover) / ISBN 978-1-250-10662-9 (ebook)

Our books may be purchased in bulk for promotional, educational, or business use. Please contact your local bookseller or the Macmillan Corporate and Premium Sales Department at (800) 221-7945 ext. 5442 or by e-mail at MacmillanSpecialMarkets@macmillan.com.

Book design by Ellen Duda

Imprint logo designed by Amanda Spielman

Illustrations by Anoosha Syed

First edition, 2018

1 3 5 7 9 10 8 6 4 2

mackids.com

Steal this book and you may find
Proper words won't come to mind.
If you're asked to speak out loud
You'll sound the fool before the crowd.

For scientists past, present, and future—

true superheroes

B.H. & S.H.S.

antennae
(hidden)

seasonal
freckles

casual but
confident outfit

secret bug
powers
(not shown)

7th-grade
swagger

Amanda Price stepped up to the ledge of Oyster Cove's tallest building, the TransMutual credit union, and peered down. Twelve stories below, Emily Battfield, Amanda's ex-best friend, stood with her slender arms outstretched and a bored expression on her face. Amanda shuddered. This trust fall was going to be an absolute disaster.

Standing on the ground, Emily looked more likely to catch a cold than she was to catch her former-friend-turned-hero-partner. But Amanda's grandfather, Poppy, was insistent that "trust" was the next phase of the girls' superduo training.

"Turn around and drop!" Poppy shouted up to Amanda.

Easy for him to say, Amanda thought, though she knew he was trying to be encouraging. She took a deep breath and imagined fusilli, picturing the corkscrew noodles in her mind. Thinking about pasta to take her mind off of her fear was one of the first wacky tips Poppy had given her after her bug powers had begun to emerge. Her grandfather's instruction to focus on noodles in the face of fear had seemed totally random, but when she tried it, Amanda realized it really did distract her just enough to calm down and keep her insectile powers at bay. And Poppy had made very clear that for this exercise she was not to use her wings, or übercool exoskeleton, or any of the other powers that transformed the mild-mannered seventh grader into her amazing alter ego, Bug Girl. So she had to stay calm. And to do that, she had to think of pasta.

Poppy's little trust fall was intended to encourage bonding, team building, and, *duh*, trust. Amanda was supposed to trust Emily to keep her from splattering like a grasshopper on the windshield of a speeding car. The girls had been on a fairly relentless course of training all summer (superhuman burpees, flaming car tosses, cow lifting, Herculean parkour, and—Frida's favorite—

Lunges Around the World) and were now keeping a twice-weekly schedule. Their trainers included Poppy; their famous supermoms Dragonfly and Megawoman; and the infamous revolutionary-in-exile, Marvella Corazon, better known in Oyster Cove as Frida, the Battfields' home assistant.

The instruction had been going surprisingly well . . . until the start of school changed things. Now Bug Girl was feeling less sure of her "partner" than ever before.

It was like something got twisted when the bell rang that first day. The moment Emily set her size-six foot back inside the halls of Oyster Cove Middle School, she started acting weird—or, well, like the old Emily. It was as if that stupid bell had erased everything that happened at the end of last year; as if saving their mothers and defeating The Exterminator and going through all the relentless training meant nothing to Emily. She hadn't even bothered coming up with a superhero name for herself yet.

"Quit yer lollygagging and drop!" Poppy shouted.

Amanda glanced down at Emily once more, who looked bored and completely uninterested in preventing

summer-blond highlights

over-it expression

exfoliated glow

whatever!

fresh mani-pedi

new ensemble

secret superpowers (not shown)

Amanda's head from cracking like a melon on the pavement. Drawing a deep breath, Amanda let herself fall. She hurtled toward the ground, picking up speed. She braced for impact as best she could—fully expecting Emily to yank her arms away, step back from her catching position, and wail "Ewww" rather than have to touch her.

But, to Amanda's surprise, Emily did not move. Much. The ground raced to meet her, wind whistled in her ears, and then Amanda felt Emily's willowy arms beneath her. Her limbs were stronger than they looked. Though Emily's powers were still revealing themselves (and were more than a little unpredictable), she was ultrastrong, could shatter glass with her scream, and had the power to start an avalanche with the stomp of her feet. And she tapped into her powers most intensely when she got angry.

While Emily did manage to slow Amanda's plummeting descent, she also took pains to stretch her body as far from Amanda's as possible, as if she were catching a sack of vomit, or a filled diaper, or something else nobody wants to touch. As a result, both girls ended up on the ground with Amanda on the bottom. *Of course.*

"Thanks," Amanda grunted when Emily had rolled off of her and she could get air back into her lungs. Emily wasn't just stronger than she looked; she was heavier than she looked, too.

"What was I supposed to do? Let you fall?" Emily stood and brushed off her outfit, more concerned about dust than about Amanda, who was still struggling to breathe.

Emily turned and started walking toward the Airstream trailer Poppy had parked nearby. Amanda got to her feet and followed. The trailer was their mobile training unit. Amanda absolutely loved the camper's curved, shiny metal; it reminded her of her favorite isopods, armadillidiidae, which most people call roly-polies.

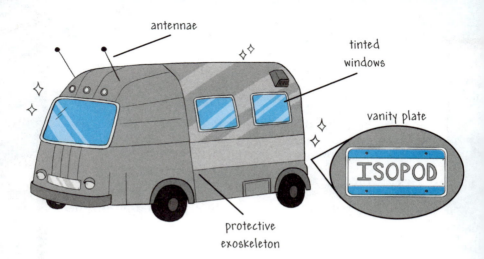

antennae

tinted windows

vanity plate

ISOPOD

protective exoskeleton

She and her best friend (and fellow science enthusiast) Vincent Verbiglia had attached silver antennae to the front end of the trailer to enhance the resemblance. It was positively adorable.

"I'm starving!" Emily announced, banging open the door to the shiny rig.

Amanda followed Emily up the steps. Poppy was on her heels, looking at his watch and mumbling about something. Amanda's grandfather insisted that the girls replenish themselves with healthy snacks and lots of water at regular intervals—though he frequently forgot what those intervals were.

Amanda was especially glad for this time-out. She was

hungry, too, and exhausted both physically and emotionally due to the insane number of lunges they'd done earlier and Emily's prickly-as-a-cactus demeanor. She needed a break—a long one—and she had a good idea about how to get it. She just had to get Poppy to make good on something he'd promised earlier in the day. . . .

Although Poppy was pretty relentless about the girls' fitness, nutrition, and safety, there were other, quirkier aspects of his personality that Amanda was counting on.

1) Poppy was prone to distraction.

   Extremely prone.

2) Poppy loved to spin yarns. Long ones.

3) Poppy had been on the scene during Megawoman and Dragonfly's golden era. After all, he was Dragonfly's father and was in charge of the duo's wardrobe and accessories in addition to being a premier sidekick in the supercircuit. In his eighty-six years, Poppy had seen and done it all—or knew the people who had.

Amanda settled on a comfortable meditation pillow with a handful of edamame while Emily leaned on the edge of the folding table and picked at a small cupful of air-popped corn.

"Poppy, tell us about one of the really nasty baddies," Amanda said, putting a bright-green bean into her mouth.

"Hmmm. Now, let me think." Poppy rubbed the stubble on his chin. Amanda could practically see him reaching back into the cobwebbed recesses of his memory.

"Ah, yes!" he exclaimed, grasping a recollection. "How about I tell you the story of Petunia Bibblesworth? She was an angry one, she was. And you probably know her by her villainess name." He paused for dramatic effect. "Frustrasia!"

Poppy was corny as cereal flakes, but when they heard the name, both girls gasped. *Frustrasia!*

Besides being generally destructive and despicable, Frustrasia was also the subject of Amanda's all-time favorite episode of her mother's hit show, *The Most Righteous Action Adventures of Dragonfly and Megawoman: Oyster Cove Defenders!* The notorious foe's antics were scandalous, and she was best known for the time she nearly destroyed Oyster Cove's upscale fashion district. Young Amanda had reenacted the battle scene with her Frustrasia action figure so vigorously and so often that the doll's head had fallen clean off.

Amanda sat back. This story was gonna be good!

Poppy stood and began to pace the length of the training trailer. He waved his hands as he told Frustrasia's origin story and changed his voice for effect. He played *all* the parts.

"'I spent four frustrated hours getting this perm!'" Poppy shrieked in a scratchy falsetto, pretending to be the hairdo-challenged troublemaker. "'And just look at my hair! Look at it! It's not curly. It's not stylish. And I *stink*!'" Poppy wailed. He held his nose. He flailed his arms in false panic and bent close to the girls so they could inspect the "damage" to his traumatized tresses (though there were not many hairs left on the actor's head).

Emily, sitting not-too-close beside Amanda, was clearly as rapt as she was, though Amanda's popularity-driven counterpart would never admit it. The scowling blonde was scarcely breathing as she moved a single piece of popcorn, in superslow-mo, from her bowl to her mouth. Amanda wished she could grab her former friend's hand and squeeze it—that the two of them could share the excitement. She wished they could exchange wide-eyed looks and delight in the story *together*. But Emily kept a chilly distance and would not make eye contact. Amanda doubted they would ever be as close as they had been before middle school. Even though, now that they were partners in fighting crime, their relationship was more important than ever.

"That bad hairdo about did poor Petunia in," Poppy said, slapping his knee. "It chapped her hide so badly that some say it's what created the heat behind Frustrasia's first devastating Vexation Ray. She started blasting green misery beams out of her eyes hither and thither! Why, she fried the giant fiberglass cow on the roof of Dribble Burgers with a glance. And the screaming and complaining!" Poppy raised his voice in a simulated wail. "'I can't possibly show myself at Shawnda's bachelorette party with my hair looking like this, can I? It's ruined!'"

"Was it really that bad?" Emily asked, her voice a whisper, her skin pale.

Amanda bit her lower lip. Losing it over a 'do was not something she could really relate to. "It's just hair," she mumbled.

"Mandy, this was not *just* hair," Poppy said, shaking his head. "What remained on Petunia's head after the coiffure disaster was a calamity. Her once boring, dishwater locks looked like sticky spaghetti with no sauce—and they worked like Medusa's snakes. Everyone who gazed upon Frustrasia's head was rendered speechless, and most of them froze right where they were. After getting an eyeful of that horror, folks couldn't even move."

Emily gulped.

Poppy shook his head gravely. He stopped pacing. He took a wide stance and looked at the girls. "But does a bad hairdo give a disappointed debutante an excuse to break every bottle in Madam Cheffae's Perfume Parlour? No, it does not! The essence of Charcuterie Number Twelve lingered in the air for months after Frustrasia's

Charcuterie
Number Twelve

terrible tantrum! Mon Dieu!" Poppy stomped his foot, shaking the trailer, then gazed out the window, his nostrils flaring at the olfactory memory. "It smelled like . . . it smelled like bacon . . . mixed with magnolia . . . coated in clam juice . . . steeped in vanilla . . . wrapped in pickled herring and left to ripen in the sun. In fact, it reminded me a little of the time I traveled above the Arctic Circle to dig up a rare Nordic delicacy—"

"But, Poppy," Amanda interrupted. "How did they defeat her? Our moms, I mean. What did they do to put a stop to Frustrasia's awful rampage?"

"Oh! Well. Your mamas arrived on the scene lickety-split. They weren't having any of Frustrasia's codswallop! Megawoman could not look directly at Frustrasia for fear of being frozen, which meant she could not use her trademark withering stare to shut down the hairdo-challenged terror. Luckily, thanks to her groovy drago-mask and insecto-vision—a little something I cooked up in Paris with famous eyewear designer Giles Bardot—Dragonfly could look directly at Frustrasia.

"Mandy, your mama hovered like a helicopter. She kept her enhanced vision focused on the lady who was losing it, while down below—proving once and for all that an accessory is never *just* an accessory—Megawoman used her belt as a blindfold. In one swoop she made a bold fashion statement, protected her eyes, and freed her body up for the work that had to be done!"

Poppy stopped to chuckle at the memory. "Those gutsy gals worked together like peanut butter and jelly. Dragonfly shouted out instructions to her girl on the ground. And Megawoman answered the call.

"With only Dragonfly's voice to guide her, Megawoman threw herself in front of Frustrasia's blasts, blocking them to protect innocents. She hurled suit racks into the villainess's path to slow her assault. Finally she doused the desperate diva in the Prêt-à-Porter fountain, drenching her 'do and extinguishing her perilous powers. The battle ended then and there. But the chemicals that devastated Frustrasia's hair took a long-lasting toll on her mind. The poor woman was never the same."

"Wow." Amanda exhaled. It didn't matter that she knew the story inside and out. It amazed her every time.

"So what happened?" Emily asked. Amanda looked at her, questioning. "To her hair, I mean," Emily added, as if it were obvious.

Poppy chuckled. "It all fell out in the fountain. Frustrasia was bald for a bit and then, when her hair grew back, it was curly. Some say that's because your mothers scared her so bad."

"Wow," Amanda said again. She shook her head at the floor, dumbfounded. Dragonfly and Megawoman were a total team. They trusted each other. They looked out for each other. They worked in harmony, like ants and bees, anticipating each other's needs and always pitching in. She leveled her gaze so she was looking right at Emily, who was picking the unpopped kernels out of her popcorn bowl and dropping them on the ground for someone else to step on or clean up.

Amanda tried to silence her doubts. It was hard. She couldn't help but wonder, *Will Emily and I* ever *be a great team?*

It sure didn't seem likely.

PILL BUG

Fun Bug Fact: Though they are referred to as bugs, these isopods are more closely related to crustaceans, like shrimp, and breathe through gills. They don't pee, their blood is blue, and they turn purple or blue when they're sick.

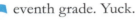

Seventh grade. Yuck.

School had been in session at Oyster Cove Middle School for exactly one week, and Amanda's hope of rekindling her relationship with Emily had evaporated faster than boiling water over a Bunsen burner.

Amanda just didn't get it. She and Emily had totally teamed up to save the town—and their mothers—AND each other—from a sinister plot hatched by one of the world's most diabolical (and ancient) evil masterminds. They had worked together like partners and friends during the summer months. But now, back in school, there was an autumn chill in the air.

Emily reverted to her clique of superficial socialites on day one. Mikki Folders, Sadie Bimmins, Prissy Jo Feingold, Lorricent Grandy, and, of course, the ultranasty Calypso Jade flocked to her like moths to a porch light, and it seemed like that was going to be the norm for the rest of the year.

Amanda told herself that Emily really *did* have her reasons—if the two of them were suddenly besties again in public, eyebrows would be raised and curiosity piqued. They needed to keep it cool in order to protect their secret superhero identities.

And, truth be told, Amanda was happy to spend her school time with Vincent and other members of the Oyster Cove Entomological Society. The more withdrawn students sheltered one another from the daily onslaught of middle-school life as best they could. They were fun to hang around with. And Amanda loved talking with her supersmart friends about the most recent lessons in science and math.

But although it seemed like everyone had simply slipped back into the grueling-yet-familiar school year routine, Amanda sensed that something was amiss. The strange vibe had Amanda's sensors on mild alert. The tingling sensation in her forehead made it hard to concentrate on Mrs. Mellonnaizie's history lecture, which should have held Amanda rapt.

The tall, skinny teacher leaned on the edge of her desk as she told her class about Oyster Cove's legendary fermentation vats—the basins that bore the beginnings of the town's infamous sauerkraut and pickle industries. Amanda loved hearing about the local crock legends and their creator, Penelope Offalblog, aka the Pickle Princess.

Penelope was Oyster Cove royalty. She alone was responsible for the trend of locally jarred vegetables that put the town on the map. Even today, tourists flocked from all over to visit the now-defunct vats that looked like enormous stoneware troughs and stood proudly behind the Abel Goatslam Memorial Branch Library. The giant tubs had at one time been filled with a secret-recipe brine along with cabbage, cucumbers, and other vegetables, which fermented into batches of deliciously salty yet healthy treats.

Amanda, like most Oyster Cove youngsters, had been brought up loving sauerkraut and pickles and had visited the historic vat site frequently. The original tubs had long ago stopped fermenting probiotic treats, but Amanda always thought she could still smell their lingering vinegary goodness.

Happily, after the Pickle Princess retired, locals leaped on the bandwagon, creating copycat batches of pickled vegetables (and sometimes eggs!) in their own small containers to sell at the farmers' market near the vat site and thus continuing Oyster Cove's briny tradition.

Just hearing the story in class was making Amanda hungry. She was wondering if Poppy had packed her any kimchi for lunch when she felt a twinge of distress radiate through her concealed antennae. She squirmed in her seat. The probiotic lecture was engaging, but her investigative urge was stronger.

When the bell rang, Amanda practically flew out the door. Her feelers and her stomach told her to scamper straight to the cafeteria. Luckily, it was her lunch period, so she didn't have to risk terror at the hands of Sandra Slivverwort, the school's meanest hall monitor. And she had forty-five minutes to conduct her investigation.

By the time Amanda burst into the lunchroom, her antennae were practically screaming. And with good reason.

She was assaulted by two things: 1) the overpowering aroma of onions and feet, and 2) a group of downtrodden students lined up against the far wall by the windows. At the front of the line was Geraldine Atrixious, or Geri, as she preferred to be called. Amanda had predicted that the prissy new girl would be trouble the moment she minced her way into a seventh-grade classroom. But worse was that right behind Geri stood . . .

Emily.

"Next," Geri called haughtily. When she snapped her fingers, a sad-eyed sixth-grade boy shuffled away from the wall and stood before her. Geri looked him up and down slowly. Then she whipped out a pad and furiously scribbled a lengthy note before ripping the sheet off, handing it to the boy, and sending him on his way.

Amanda watched, perplexed. She had no idea what was going on, but when she spotted Vincent in the line,

shiny bob

insulting sneer

pretentious bauble

fashion ticket book

fashionista romper

beach-ready tan

kitten heels

looking miserable and anxious, she went over to stand beside him.

"Vincent, what on earth is happening?" Amanda whispered.

"*She*'s happening. *Her.* Geri." Vincent pointed to the nastiness at the head of the line. "She was waiting when we got here, and she made us all line up. She said it's mandatory—before we can eat lunch. Emily was with her, and they both looked too scary to say no to. So . . . I don't know what it's about, but I hope it's over soon. I'm starving."

Amanda got into line. Keeping one eye on Geri and Emily, she tried to distract Vincent from his hunger pangs and general nervousness by chatting about their science assignment for Mr. Schenkenclabber's class. Slowly, they inched forward. When they finally got to the front, Geri stared at Vincent.

"Fashion ticket," she hissed, looking at Vincent's meticulously prepared ensemble and checking off boxes on her pad. "Review this document and make sure never to violate the codes listed on it again." She ripped off the ticket and thrust it at Vincent.

The startled boy's eyebrows arched into perfect *V*s. "I beg your pardon," he spat. "My outfits faultlessly blend retro and current fashions. If you think this outfit is a violation, then the problem is *you*." He reviewed the ticket. "Puh-lease! These are NOT flares!" he shouted, pushing past the nasty Geri and giving Emily a sad glance.

Amanda watched, aghast. Insulting Vincent's always-impeccable attire was preposterous. But what really cheesed her was Emily. Popular or not, how could she just stand there and let this new— albeit rather glamorous-looking—girl insult Vincent without even lifting a manicured finger to protest? Vincent had practically saved Emily's life during their battle with The Exterminator, and yet there she was, allowing some

Fashion Ticket

- ☑ too small
- ☐ too big
- ☑ matchy-matchy
- ☑ flares
- ☐ prints and patterns
- ☐ sandals and socks
- ☐ failure to iron
- ☐ worn, torn, or stained
- ☐ sweater-tucking
- ☐ hippie rubbish
- ☑ très passé
- ☐ accessory catastrophe
- ☐ hand-me-down disaster
- ☐ dreary
- ☐ turtleneck
- ☐ high-waters
- ☐ laundry day calamity
- ☐ just no

Write-Ins:

_____
_____
_____

Signature:
Geraldine Atrixious

self-proclaimed fashion officer to totally treat him like trash! It was unacceptable, even for Emily.

"And you," Geri said, giving Amanda a side-eyed glance, "are beyond hope. Maybe I'll have time to write you up later, in science class."

Amanda could only manage a nasty look as she hurried after Vincent.

"I cannot believe her!" Amanda fumed when she caught up to her friend.

Amanda and Vincent took their seats at the unofficial Oyster Cove Entomological Society table, opened their lunches, and chewed in silence as they watched Geri continue her abuse. Vincent's outburst hadn't fazed her in the least. She assessed student after student with her cold stare, finding each one wanting in their wardrobe choices and issuing them tickets detailing their fashion missteps. Before long, everyone in the lunchroom looked as if they might burst into tears.

"Where did Geri come from, anyway?" Amanda finally asked, angrily chomping on the falafel ball Poppy had packed for her.

"She's in my math class," Sh'Shelle Domalie answered. "On the first day, she stood up to introduce herself. She told us she's a transfer student from Lethargy Point Academy and then announced 'who' she was wearing.

"'Oh, DO call me Geri,'" Sh'Shelle mimicked, pursing her lips. "'That's my nickname. Isn't it darling?'"

She paused for effect and then leaned in. "She's capital-*T* trouble, mark my words. She makes Emily look positively pleasant! And have you noticed? The two are never apart."

Amanda had noticed, but she was trying not to be bothered by it. In a way, it made perfect sense that Emily had glommed on to this new girl like a barnacle on to the hull of a ship. Mean girls travel in packs. It's just that Amanda had hoped that Emily was moving on from that kind of thing.

For a brief moment Amanda dared to hope that maybe Emily was siding with this new girl as a way to help keep their secret identities safe. Or to protect the other OCMS students from Geri's wrath. No superhero would voluntarily hang out with someone so cruel! Except maybe her "partner," who stood behind Geri without flinching while the new girl doled out insults.

Amanda put away the rest of her meal. She'd lost her appetite. Emily may have been a hero in the battle against The Exterminator, but it appeared that seventh grade would see her teaming up with the enemy. Amanda sighed loudly in disappointment.

And then the screaming began.

3

The otherworldly screech was radiating from none other than Geri's perfectly glossed piehole. Sure, Geri was cute with her shiny bob, fashionista romper, and kitten heels, but did she need to commandeer the entire lunch period with her nasty shenanigans *and* awful shrieking?

Amanda expected Geri to be wailing over a tucked-in sweater or an overly short hem, but the girl's caterwauling was caused by the brown lump of FDA–approved food-stuff the cafeteria lady had plopped onto her lunch tray. Yes, it looked like boiled chicken skin in sauce, but it was lunch, and, in fact, Amanda thought it appeared down-right appealing compared to some of the other slop she'd seen served in the cafeteria.

Geri, beet-red with rage, was voicing her horror at a disinterested cafeteria worker whose hairnet dangled precariously atop a tuft of graying and knotted hair. The

alleged vegetable
(boiled beyond recognition)

gelatinous goo

"chocolate cake"

gray meat

worker had been serving snotty kids the same viscous nonfoods for nearly thirty years and had stopped caring almost as long ago.

"What *is* this pile of lipids?" Geri yowled, pointing at the gelatinous and foaming puddle that had been dumped onto her plate next to a slice of what one could only assume was chocolate cake. (Although, it looked more like a dried sponge speckled with coffee grounds.)

"It's called Hobo Stew," the worker replied. "Potatoes, some kind of beef thing. Maybe it's beef. . . . Who knows these days?"

The new girl flinched. "Am I seriously supposed to *eat* this?"

"I just serve it; I don't cook it," the worker wheezed.

"If you want to lodge a complaint, take it up with Hoagie Joe back there. *He's* the cook."

With that, the worker thrust a wooden spoon—thickly encrusted with brownish, chunky residue—toward the kitchen. There stood a giant, unshaven oaf who looked like he ate children for lunch instead of cooking lunch for children.

"Got a problem with it, kid?" Hoagie Joe growled. "Get back here and get cooking. Otherwise, can it. I got meat to boil." He menacingly brandished a decades-old ladle.

The new girl, apparently startled by the cook's attitude, suddenly became quiet. She picked up her tray and carried it stiffly away from the lunch line.

Amanda and Vincent witnessed the whole exchange from the safety

hairnet

angry glare

spoon caked
with lunches
of yesteryear

five o'clock
shadow

dirty
apron

leftovers

of their table. Not many kids ever got vocal with the lunch lady, let alone the cook, who'd served them this slop in the sixth grade as well. This was big news. As they sat with their mouths open, gaping, Geri strode past holding her tray as far away from her body as possible.

"What are you looking at, Frumpalong Cassidy?" she snipped at Amanda, giving a very judgmental full-body scan. "Thrift Plus called—they've recalled that shirt because they're embarrassed they ever sold it."

Amanda's antennae smarted. She squeezed her eyes shut and thought of spaghetti to try to short-circuit her impulses. Feeling her sensilla relax, she opened her eyes to follow the new girl's snotty path across the cafeteria. Students parted before her, anticipating her every move, allowing her to go wherever she wanted. Behind her, Emily and her gaggle of cronies fell in line.

Geri sashayed to an empty table and set down her tray. Gingerly, she placed the brown spongiform mass to the side and nibbled lazily at an apple, the one seemingly edible portion of her lunch. She did not look at any of the students who were blatantly staring at her. She didn't attempt to engage anyone in conversation. Once she was finished with her apple, she turned to a trembling nerd attempting to pass by unnoticed.

"Take my tray up," she ordered the petrified adolescent. Without pause, she passed her tray to him, slime and all. She then got up, swanned through the throng to the front of the cafeteria, stopped, and turned. She appeared to be surveying the landscape, transferring her gaze from table to table, and judging each. Some groups of students made her groan in disgust, other packs she simply ignored. One or two cliques made her pause. Amanda thought she saw a flicker of interest in the girl's cold, green eyes as she completed her survey of Emily and the rest of the clique she'd just been sitting with. But before Amanda could decipher the look, Geri turned on her heel and walked out the door, leaving the entire student body sitting in stunned silence.

Once it was evident that Geri would not be returning, all of the students burst into simultaneous chatter. Soon the cafeteria was humming like a hive of bees.

"I'm gonna barf," Amanda whispered to Vincent as they shuffled toward the trash cans to dispose of their lunch waste. Amanda didn't need any more distractions in her life right now, and she could tell from Emily's interest in this new girl that things were about to get even more unpleasant.

"The last thing we need right now," Amanda whispered to Vincent as they walked out of the cafeteria, "is another nasty girl in this school treating everyone like garbage. When does it end?"

As if to prove Amanda's point, when the two stepped  into the hallway, they heard sobbing. It took a moment, but finally they located the source—a weeping student was slumped beside the water fountain. She blended in so well that Amanda might have mistaken her for a pile of backpacks if she hadn't heard the snuffling. She pointed and Vincent nodded. He saw her, too.

Neither of them recognized the girl, but that didn't stop them from being concerned.

"Hi," Amanda said. "Are you all right?" She offered a hand and helped the crying girl up.

"I'm fine," the girl sniffled. "It's just . . . I try so hard to blend in. I don't want to call attention to myself. And then . . . well, I just got this ticket." She took a quivering breath. "According to this, I'm not allowed to wear turtlenecks to school anymore. Look." She held out the fashion ticket. Amanda looked at it over Vincent's shoulder. Geri had checked nearly every box on the sheet and even written one in that said simply, "Dump." And it was checked, too.

"Well," Vincent said reassuringly, "these fashion tickets are hardly official. They're just cruel! I mean, she gave *me* one. And just look at this outfit!" He turned so Amanda and the crying girl could get the full effect, using his hands to highlight his favorite parts.

"Yeah," Amanda added. "She's just being a bully!" Amanda stuck out her hand again, this time for a proper introduction. "I don't think we've officially met. I'm Amanda."

"Hi," the sniffling student said. "We've been in classes

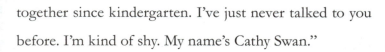

together since kindergarten. I've just never talked to you before. I'm kind of shy. My name's Cathy Swan."

Vincent and Amanda looked at each other, then they looked back at Cathy, then back at each other. Amanda thought the name sounded familiar—like she had heard it during roll call—and wondered how it was possible that she had never spoken to this girl before.

"I don't socialize much, but I have a rich inner life," Cathy said, as if reading Amanda's thoughts. She shrugged. "Plus I bake a lot. It's my hobby. And it's rather time-consuming. Do you want a raspberry-maple-macadamia-white-chocolate-fudge biscotti?" She reached into her backpack, fishing for something way down at the bottom.

Before Amanda could accept any baked goods or ask any more questions or even introduce Cathy to the rest of the Oyster Cove Entomological Society—the group had joined them in the hall—the crew was interrupted by a loud hum, a pop, and the annoying crackle of a megaphone.

4

"Cryptid sighting! Cryptid sighting!" Nafario Dwillings shouted into his handheld amplifier as he marched down the halls of OCMS toward Amanda and her friends. Nafario, the self-appointed student newscaster, believed it was his duty to scream updates to the student body whenever he felt a local happening or a tidbit of gossip was hot enough. The updates were convenient, if annoying.

"What's a cryptid?" Sh'Shelle shouted after the walking information desk. But she was too late; Nafario rounded the corner, moving away from the cluster of self-described science geeks, taking his megaphone and breaking news to parts unknown.

As Nafario's amplified voice faded, Vincent cleared his throat and answered Sh'Shelle's question himself. "A cryptid," he explained, "is a monster or animal that people claim to have seen even though there is no scientific proof of its existence."

Everyone, including Cathy, turned to face the pint-size smarty-pants. Amanda smiled. Vincent was starting to enjoy having an audience.

"For example," Vincent went on, "Bigfoot has been spotted in forests around the country for decades, though never captured. And then of course there's the Loch Ness Monster of Scotland, perhaps the most famous cryptid in the world. The monster of the loch, or 'Nessie,' as she is known, has racked up sightings for centuries, and the most popular theory is that she must be a plesiosaur—a throwback from the Mesozoic Era."

Amanda was familiar with Vincent's deep knowledge of cryptozoology but was still impressed by what her friend could spout from memory. The rest of the group listened in awe. A few of them even began to take notes as Vincent moved from the more famous elusive beings to local legends such as the Marzipan Beast of Crackerfield Flats—a creature that purportedly looked like a cross between a human and a lemur.

"This beast is absolutely obsessed with marzipan," Vincent explained. "It has been known to break into specialty food shops around Crackerfield Flats. There's been fuzzy footage caught on security cameras (and a lot of marzipan consumed) but, like the other cryptids, the creature has never been caught."

Sh'Shelle listened, agape. Amanda, worried the girl might drool, gave Vincent a raised eyebrow to hint that he should wrap up his lecture.

"But whether Mr. Marzipan was really a monster or just some thief in a costume who was crazy about almond paste, no one can be certain," Vincent concluded.

"So what's this thing Nafario's talking about?" Amanda asked. Before her recent changes, Amanda would have shrugged off talk of mythic local monsters as wishful thinking. But ever since her own . . . evolution . . . she was open to the idea that some things just plain defy explanation.

"Oh. Right. Well, yesterday, Darnell Hausfrau sent a video to channel 4, WTOC, of some footage he took at Rickets Lake," Vincent explained. "The cryptid in

CRYPTIDS

Name	Description	Location
Loch Ness Monster	Plesiosaur	Scotland
Bigfoot/Sasquatch	Enormous ape-man	US and Canadian Pacific Northwest
Chupacabra	Lizard-like bipedal goat-sucker	Central and South America/Southern US/Puerto Rico
Jersey Devil	Winged bipedal horse	New Jersey
Jackalope	Horned rabbit	Wyoming and Western US
Yeti	White ape	Himalayas
Ogopogo	Lake serpent	British Columbia
Marzipan Beast	Hairy humanoid	Crackerfield Flats
Qilin	Dragon-like chimera	China
Minhocão	Giant earthworm	South and Central America
Rickie	Unknown	Oyster Cove

question, should it exist, is our very own lake monster. I believe the anchorperson referred to the creature as 'Rickie.'"

"Rickie, huh? So what does Rickie look like?" Amanda asked, tilting her head a bit.

"Naturally, like all cryptid footage, the image was pretty blurry," Vincent said, "but from what I saw on the news segment, he looked like a slimy, blue-green, soft-shell turtle. He romped around the lake for a few seconds and then he disappeared."

Vincent looked up and down the hall, scanning for monitors, and then pulled out his phone. He tapped at it before turning the screen around. "Darnell did manage to capture photos of some pretty interesting muddy footprints," he told the crew. "I was planning to go see the evidence for myself after school."

Amanda leaned in. A hot dog had been placed next to a pair of large, muddy impressions in the ground so that viewers could get a sense of the size. The prints were about two feet long, with froglike webbed feet. *Impressive.* But easy to fake.

Vincent swiped the screen to a new image. It showed curious townsfolk, news vans, and cameras waiting on the muddy banks for Rickie to make another appearance. The crowd lined the shore, which was weird, because Rickets Lake was usually abandoned. Nobody went near *that* quagmire of pollution unless they had to.

Referred to by local officials as a "water rehabilitation facility," it was made up of sludge from old drainage pipes, foul black water, and stringy, murky pockets of noxious sewage. The "lake" sat behind an abandoned shopping center on South Clam Lane, and was second only to Armpit Acres (the town landfill) in its ability to cause nausea in passersby.

Once upon a time, Rickets Lake had been beautiful, clear, and surrounded by pastoral hills. That was before building began on the Shoppes at South Clam. Workers had dumped toxic materials from construction into the water instead of disposing of them properly. Once the lake was destroyed, others began unloading their awful refuse there as well. Chemicals of all kinds had been drained into the waters until the place was declared a toxic waste site, off-limits and devoid of life. It was abandoned, left for time and nature to sort out—a project that could take millennia. Rumor had it that if you stuck your finger in Rickets Lake's fetid water, you'd pull back nothing but bone!

Amanda shuddered to think of what poor creature could be living in that nasty, tarlike liquid. "If there is a Rickie living in Rickets Lake, we've got to help him!" she cried. "No creature should be forced to survive in such atrocious conditions. He's probably being poisoned!" Amanda's mind was spinning. She was outraged and so intent on putting together a rescue mission that she forgot all about the lunchroom debacle and hallway bullying until she spotted Geri, Emily, and the rest of the popular set coming toward them . . . again.

Cathy had noticed the approaching flock and wedged herself behind the water fountain, where she would be out of sight.

"What's all this about a tacky bog beast?" Geri hissed to her newly assembled entourage. The girls all giggled, and Prissy Jo Feingold snorted. Embarrassed, she pretended to cough.

"Unexplained phenomena are just plain gauche," Geri pronounced.

"Yeah. I bet it's ugly," Yelba Marcos added. "It's probably hiding in that yuck because no one wants to look at it."

"Speaking of yuck, has anyone seen Cathy Swan? I need to revise her ticket. Polyester stretch pants require a second check in the DON'T box," Geri cooed viciously. The girls all giggled again as they walked past the Entomological Society without giving them a glance. Amanda had a sick ache in her stomach that had nothing to do with her bug powers and everything to do with how mean Geri was. She crouched beside the water fountain and offered Cathy her hand once more, admiring how well the colors in the timid girl's outfit blended with the bland neutrals of the school walls—tepid taupe, muted mint, beige. It was impressive camouflage. It reminded her of the way the copper underwing's appearance merged with tree bark—making it almost disappear.

"She's gone now," Amanda said gently, accepting the biscotti—an Italian double-baked treat—that Cathy held out to her. She smiled encouragingly, but she could sense that the danger for Cathy wasn't over. Geri had targeted the near-invisible girl for nastiness.

Amanda could not let that stand.

But first she needed to address this lake monster situation. "About Rickie—"

"Begging your pardon," Vincent interrupted, tapping his Casio calculator watch, "but we have to table this convo for a later time. We have got to get to class pronto!"

"Okay. Yes. Right," Amanda said. She waved goodbye to Cathy as Vincent pulled her toward their fourth-period commitments. "Meet by the fountain after school," she called over her shoulder to her fellow science geeks. "We need to come up with a plan!"

COPPER UNDERWING

Fun Bug Fact: Moths like the copper under-wing are often gray and brown in hue. Their coloring helps them blend in with the bark of trees and shrubs—and avoid getting eaten!

5

For almost three whole months, Tuesdays had been Amanda's favorite day of the week. Ever since she and Emily had pulled off the great rescue of Dragonfly and Megawoman, they, along with their moms and the indispensable Frida and Poppy, had held weekly meetings over a dinner of tacos beside the Battfields' pool. It was part training and part fiesta, and it gave them all a chance to touch base.

In addition to being tasty, the Taco Tuesday ritual made Amanda feel hopeful, like she was part of something bigger. When the supercrew gathered around the table, they turned into something much greater than the sum of their parts; not just salsa and beans and spicy filling in a warm corn tortilla . . . but a taco! A perfect handheld meal. A pocket of deliciousness! A winning combination! A team!

It was at those moments—maybe because Emily was always on her best behavior in front of her mom—that Amanda truly believed she and Emily would find a way to work together and make a difference. It was on Tuesdays, after Frida's weekly lecture on revolutionists and before Poppy brought out his famous flan, that Amanda actually felt like they were bonding.

In fact, only a few weeks prior, the girls had a long talk about their emerging powers—wondering what their limits were, what abilities might develop next, and when they would know they were done, you know . . . changing. Emily had even confessed to Amanda that she was struggling to choose a supername.

"It's just . . . kind of a big deal," Emily had confided nervously. "I can't simply pull a name off the shelf, like It Girl, or Moxie, or Ms. Thing. I'm Megawoman's daughter. I need something . . . mega."

Amanda remembered feeling kind of warm inside when Emily had told her that. It seemed like something you would tell a partner or even a friend. It seemed right that they would share in figuring out who they were together.

But that was before. In just a handful of days, the magic of summer and salsa fresca had abruptly faded, leaving Emily to stew in silence while Amanda chewed a tortilla chip beside her, afraid to even speak.

Not that she didn't have stuff to say. There was a *lot* that Amanda wanted to say, starting with "What happened to you?" and "How can you hang around that awful, mean new girl?" But every time she opened her mouth to ask a question, she found herself stuffing guacamole into it instead. To be perfectly honest, Emily didn't need a super-name to be intimidating. She just was.

On the other side of the patio table, Frida and Poppy had their heads bent together, oblivious to the wedge growing between the girls. They'd been talking in low voices ever since Frida finished her weekly lecture on revolutionists.

Amanda always liked Frida's lessons. As a rebel fighter, she had seen a lot in her native country—and she had inspired a female uprising so successful that the government was still looking for her. Today, when she was telling them about Linda Terrible—the masked avenger who had

WANTED

BY ORDER OF THE STATE

MARVELLA CORAZON

For the crimes of: freedom-fighting, believing in equality, and inspiring others.

Beware her loyal army of rebellious women!

led the Mujeres Fuertes Strike of '94 in a battle for clean drinking water—Amanda had wondered about Frida's own alter ego, Marvella Corazon. Frida rarely discussed her past.

Amanda looked around for her mom. She spotted her coming out of the Battfields' house, her watermelon agua fresca held high and Emily's mom at her side.

"Listen up, everyone!" Charlotte Battfield said loudly, flashing her million-dollar smile. "We have an announcement!" Emily's mom, who *always* looked impeccable, was ever-so-slightly flushed.

"We're going on a trip!" Karen Price proclaimed, clapping her hands together.

For a brief moment, Amanda felt her heart lighten. A getaway was a great idea! Sure, school was barely back in session, but she was already up for a vacation. . . . But then, as her mom joined hands with Charlotte, Amanda understood that *she* was not a part of the *we*.

"It's the best news," Amanda's mom said. "The annual Heroes of the World Battle-Preparedness Symposium and Convention is happening in Cuttledale this year, and we're going to go! One of the presenters had to drop out last minute, and we've been asked to fill in with a workshop on how to maintain healthy work relationships in perilous situations. It'll be like a reunion tour!"

The two women exchanged happy glances. After being in hiding for thirteen years to protect their children, the premier Diva Duo was ready to make a comeback. And they should. But . . .

Amanda struggled to swallow the taco bite in her mouth. "But what will . . . ?"

"Poppy will stay with you, Apple Blossom," Amanda's mom said, putting a hand on her daughter's shoulder.

"And Frida will be here for you," Mrs. Battfield said. "And we'll be back before you know it!"

Emily refused to look directly at her mother.

Amanda tried to smile.

"You'll hardly even miss us, Doodle," Amanda's mom whispered, close to her daughter's ear.

Amanda looked at Emily, who was scowling at the ground. She looked at Poppy, who was still whispering to Frida—not even paying attention to the announcement. She looked at her half-eaten taco. "When do you leave?" she asked.

"In the morning!" the two moms proclaimed.

HEROES OF THE WORLD
BATTLE-PREPAREDNESS
SYMPOSIUM AND CONVENTION!

★ Superheroic panels!   ★ Vendors with all the latest supergear!   ★ No supervillains allowed!

SPECIAL GUESTS:
MEGAWOMAN
AND DRAGONFLY

This September! At the Cuttledale Convention Center and Historic Cuttlefishery!
All proceeds benefit the Cuttledale Mollusk Nursery and Rehabilitation Clinic!

On Wednesday, Amanda packed her school bag carefully. It was going to be a long day. "Dinner might be a little late," she told Trina, her Madagascar hissing cockroach. Trina didn't complain. She was a perfect pet: sweet, docile, and neat, like the rest of the multi-legged pets that filled Amanda's room. Amanda would never understand why more people didn't keep cockroaches, or spiders, or millipedes, or any of the other wonderful crawlies she adored. But there were lots of things Amanda didn't understand about most people.

Shouldering her bag, Amanda skipped downstairs. Poppy's famous breakfast chia bars were waiting on the counter, but the kitchen was empty. She found Poppy in the living room wearing a smoking jacket and goggles and watching the morning news.

Horace Rucksack was reporting from the fetid shores

of Rickets Lake, where activity had really picked up. The camera showed droves of people with binoculars, cameras, folding chairs, and giant-size snacks, all waiting to catch a glimpse of Rickie. There were other film crews as well and stands selling Rickie trinkets, T-shirts, swim trunks, and noisemakers. Amanda shook her head. The huge clapping hands, air horns, and vuvuzelas might be appropriate at a sporting event, but they were sure to frighten any wild creature. If the poisoned lake didn't do Rickie in, his new-found fans just might!

"In spite of the adoring crowds assembled here beside Rickie's home," Horace reported, "the town mascot has not shown so much as a flipper since he was first spotted."

"'In spite of'?!" Poppy scoffed. "Because of! That crowd would scare the scales off a fish!"

It was true. The throng was loud and huge, and it was littering the area with junk food wrappers. The sight made Amanda want to run back upstairs and curl up in her bed. But that was not an option for Bug Girl.

"Oh, Cabbage Blossom! There you are!" Amanda's mom rushed into the living room, shoving an enormous,

overflowing suitcase in front of her with her foot. "I was hoping I'd get to say goodbye." She hoisted the overfilled case and gave it a quick, hug-like squeeze. The clothing inside yielded and, with a click, the case was latched. With any luck, it wouldn't be picked for random search; closing that thing was way beyond the power of any airline agent!

Her mother turned and squeezed Amanda more gently. "Have a great time while I'm gone, Plum Bucket. I'll miss you."

"Mom, I really wish you weren't leaving," Amanda said. She swallowed the lump that started to come up in her throat. "I don't know if I'm ready to do this hero stuff without you."

Her mother let go of her suitcase and knelt down.

"Lotus Blossom," her mom said, "I know how tough this transition can be. I was there when I was your age, and I had just as many questions and doubts as you do. But just look at what you've accomplished already. You saved me and the whole town from one of the most sinister villains ever!"

Amanda sighed. "But how do I know I can do that again? What if there's a situation I can't figure out, or what if I'm not strong enough when the time comes?" She plunked down onto the couch. "And Emily isn't helping."

"Do you want to know a secret?" Amanda's mom asked, taking a seat next to her. "When I first started out, I was confused and upset. I wasn't sure of what I could do. I wanted to run and hide. And do you know who helped me get through it?"

"Poppy?" Amanda guessed.

"Nope," her mom replied. "Emily's mom. She saw things in me that I couldn't see myself, and she never gave up on me. And you know what? I finally realized that she was right—I had the strength and power to fight for justice. It was in me all along, and I just needed to believe."

Amanda shifted. "But it's so hard to talk to Emily. It's impossible!"

"Nothing's impossible, sweetie. You and Emily are the future. You need to be a friend to her like her mom was to me. It will be worth it, you'll see."

With that, Amanda's mom kissed her on the cheek and stood up to leave. "You have fun while I'm gone, okay?" she said as she pulled her suitcase out the door.

Amanda mustered a smile and a wave. This day already felt like it wasn't going to come anywhere close to good, and she didn't expect that the week ahead would be any better.

When Amanda arrived at school, she immediately had to put Poppy's pasta training to use again. She conjured up ravioli; images of plump, steaming pasta pockets floated through her mind and allowed her to keep her antennae, armor, and wings under wraps. She'd been getting pretty good at controlling her powers, both summoning and deactivating them at will. But the atmosphere at OCMS had gone beyond unnerving. Something in the hallways felt entirely sinister and was making her supersystems react involuntarily.

A sharp, stabbing pain—like a brain freeze—made her wince, and when she opened her eyes, she groaned. She should have known. Geri was walking toward her, trailing her so-called friends. She had her fashion ticket book and a permanent marker in hand and was scanning the area for her next target.

Glancing down at her outfit, Amanda thought she was pretty safe. Overalls were in right now. And Vincent told her that basketball sneakers were classic. She scanned the halls twice, then saw where Geri was headed. Cathy Swan had squeezed herself in between two of the trophy cases that lined the walls near the school's main office. And she was wearing a boxy T-shirt with a glossy iron-on proclaiming *Rickie Lives!*

In spite of Cathy's best attempt at invisibility, Geri had spotted her.

"Oh dear," Geri said, smiling viciously. "Is this strike three? One more ticket and you'll have to wear Hefty garbage bags to school! Or maybe you should just stop coming. Because nobody wants to see"—she waved her hand up and down, indicating *all* of Cathy—"this."

Amanda closed her eyes briefly and pictured herself wrapped entirely in spaghetti—like a noodle mummy. Then she stepped between Geri and Cathy, hoping the image in her head would be enough to keep her alter ego at bay. She could not abide this bullying. She could not and would not. If she couldn't stand up to it as Bug Girl, she would do it as Amanda Price!

"I like your shirt, Cathy," she said, her voice wavering. She kept her back to Geri but could feel the judgmental girl's stare. "I'm a Rickie fan, too. My friends and I are going to Rickets Lake later to conduct an investigation. Do you want to come?"

Cathy was trembling and glancing nervously over Amanda's shoulder. She managed to nod, just a bit.

"I'll bring some cranberry-chocolate-chip loaf," Cathy whispered. Then she skittered away like one of those tiny crabs on the beach that races for shelter the second it's uncovered by the tide.

"See you after school!" Amanda called. Then the smile melted off her face and she turned, slowly, to look at Geri and her entourage. "Mmm, loaf!"

Geri glowered, her lip curling. She crumpled the fashion ticket she'd been unable to issue and dropped it on the floor. It bounced off Amanda's toe. Amanda stared at the refuse. She hated litterbugs—and never understood why they were called that. Bugs would never do anything as distasteful as throwing their trash around. Bugs were world-class cleaners.

"You're . . . annoying me," Geri said, her eyes narrowing. "Like a little gnat." She enunciated overdramatically, as if she were in a bad community-theater play.

Amanda didn't flinch. She looked past Geri to examine the faces of the girls clustering around her. She actually hoped she would see Emily there. She hoped that Emily might have her back this time—that she might stand up to this mean girl's beastly behavior. That she might stand up for Amanda.

But Emily wasn't there.

Amanda scanned the crowd again. Emily wasn't the only one missing. Sadie Bimmins's sour face was missing, too. And where was Lorricent Grandy? The in-crowd was thinner than usual.

Geri looked like she was about to say something more—or take her big permanent marker and scribble on Amanda's face—but luckily, just then the bell rang, indicating that they were all late for class.

"This isn't over, you little gnat," Geri spat before hurrying down the hall.

Amanda let out a breath. *Nope.* She silently agreed, *It's not over by a long shot.*

7

When the bell finally rang at the end of the day, Amanda breathed a huge sigh of relief. Not only was the atmosphere at OCMS horrid—what with everyone scrambling around trying to avoid fashion tickets— but she was anxious to take action on this Rickie issue. Amanda was all about action.

On the walk to the lake, she doled out assignments to the entire Entomological Society. Delegation was crucial.

"Sh'Shelle, you and Stuart start by getting some water samples," Amanda directed. "We'll need to analyze those. Be sure to wear gloves." Stuart Rigby tried to salute, but he was carrying a crazy amount of gear and ended up dropping his core sample kit.

"On it," Sh'Shelle answered. She hauled a pair of bright-yellow rubber gloves out of her backpack and twirled them around. "I came prepared."

"I'll get some snaps," Vincent offered. "I've got a great eye. And the goods." He held up the two cameras he had slung around his slim neck. "Plus I can get high-res photos on my phone."

Amanda nodded. She looked at her team and finally spotted Cathy at the back of the pack; she was nearly invisible, as always. "Cathy, you and the Paganelli twins can help spot. We'll need lots of eyes on the lake if we're going to catch sight of this critter, let alone capture an image." The twins reluctantly put away the books they were always reading and gazed at the lake.

Cathy nodded. "I was out of that loaf I told you about, but I brought coconut-cinnamon-aquafaba macarons." She pulled out a plastic container.

"Ooh, I'll eat one of those macarons," Vincent said. "I love a good macaron! And I've been hankering to try aquafaba."

A smile flickered across Cathy's face as she passed one of her gourmet treats to Vincent, but it disappeared as they crested the hill.

"Excuse me, but could you people monitor your

trash?" Amanda shouted at the lazy crowd as someone dropped a potato-chip bag on the ground in front of her. "I mean, *come on.*"

The sight before them was a lot like what Amanda had already seen on TV that morning: a ridiculous display of rubbish and rubberneckers. Lookie-loos lined the mucky shoreline, wandering through the piles of broken furniture, pallets, fencing, and pipes that created a treacherous maze around the water. The crowd had brought out and

set up cheap folding chairs, sunshades, and tents. The ground around the camps was littered with empty bottles and cans and other cast-off scraps. Along the edges were large booths hawking Rickie swag, stocked with shirts, mugs, caps, posters, erasers, toilet paper cozies, and more. And there was also a smell.

Amanda covered her nose. Cabbage, bus fumes, grease traps. Apparently it was a scent people grew used

to, because the funk was not keeping the spectators away. It smelled like a combo of all of these things and more—a toxic potion that made Amanda feel barfy. But no matter—she had a mission that no stink could keep her from!

While the rest of the entomological squad set to work, Amanda circled the lake, checking the ground, the water, and even the sky for anything unusual. Long before she'd gotten souped-up insect senses, Amanda had prided herself on her keen powers of observation. They were a scientific must-have. But despite her senses, she stepped carefully on the squelching shoreline and nearly tripped over Cathy, who was crouched down in a deserted spot, blending in with the green-brown beach. Amanda crouched beside her. They both stared at the infected waters in silence. The colors reminded Amanda of the frog she had raised from a tadpole last year for science. Cletus.

A lump rose in Amanda's throat as she remembered the day the class had taken their fledgling frogs out to the fresh, clean pond behind the school and released them. Cletus had hopped from her hand. Leaping once. Twice. Then, Amanda swore, he had looked back with large, wet eyes. "Go," she'd whispered, because captivity was no place for a frog. "Be strong." Cletus had hopped away then. But not a day had passed that Amanda hadn't thought of her moist and tender ward.

Unzipping her backpack, Amanda pulled out a plastic package. *Cricket Crispies*, the label read. They were a special treat she had purchased for her amphibious friend. She couldn't bring herself to throw away the leftovers after Cletus was released. She felt too sorry for the cute little crickets that had been sacrificed to make the frog crackers and hadn't wanted them to go to waste. But just as she'd told Cletus back in sixth grade—nature is hard.

"I don't think there's any oxygen in that water," Amanda said to Cathy after a few moments. "No oxygen means no food. No food means no survivors."

Amanda crunched up a few handfuls of crispies and sprinkled them on the ground.

Amanda stared at the water, deep in thought.

There had, reportedly, been cleanup efforts way back when. But they obviously hadn't done a lick of good. It's not easy to clean water; you can't just add soap. But there had to be something Amanda and her friends could do to improve the conditions of Rickets Lake.

"Amanda," Cathy almost whispered, breaking the silence. "Thank you for inviting me. This is fun." She nibbled on one of her baked treats.

Slowly the others drifted over to where Cathy and Amanda were keeping watch. They'd gotten their water and soil samples, and Vincent had captured some images, but none were the photos of the thing they'd truly hoped to see. Amanda didn't want to say it, but she felt pretty sure that *nothing* could be living in that cesspool. She was about to open her mouth and let her fellow entomologists down easy when Cathy gasped and pointed. They all turned toward the center of the lake.

There was a ripple. Then a slippery-looking back, or fin, or tail, or tentacle broke the surface. The creature disappeared completely and then reemerged, this time coming all the way out of the water to perform a twisting leap!

In the swirling chaos of water plumes, glistening reflections, and amphibious speed, it was difficult to tell much about the mystery beast; just that it was greenish and the size of a bus. With a giant *SPLASH* the massive critter flopped back down. Water, scum, and all manner of trash rained down on the onlookers. Some screamed in horror. Some who had been in the splash zone looked like they'd been doused in pure black tar. They moaned and cursed, trying to smear the gunk off their skin. But the dismay was hard to hear over the Bug Club's ecstatic cheers.

Rickie was real. And he was alive!

8

It was getting late, and the crowds at Rickets Lake had finally started to thin. The vendors had packed up all of their hastily created wares and driven off; the newscasters had loaded up their gear; curiosity-seekers had tottered home. Only the Oyster Cove Entomological Society remained, and they were saying their good-nights.

"That was simply the most thrilling thing I've ever witnessed in my entire life," Sh'Shelle warbled. "Imagine being present for what could potentially be the unveiling of a new species!" She clasped her hands together in glee.

Stuart was more reserved. "Let's not jump to conclusions. We need to analyze all data and base our theories on fact, not emotion."

"Boring," Sh'Shelle countered. "You saw what just happened. You know that's no ordinary animal in the water."

Sh'Shelle had a point. What they had just seen was

incredible. But it was a school night, and they needed to get home. Reluctantly, everyone headed away from Rickets Lake.

Everyone, that is, except Amanda and Vincent. The two friends were too taken by the situation to simply pick up and leave, and they quietly decided to linger to see if they could sneak in a private viewing. Besides, it was nice to be away from school and the horrible maltreatment and social hierarchy there. They sat together in abandoned folding chairs, looking at the emerging stars and trying their hardest not to pass out from the tainted water's rank odor.

Vincent kept his handy night-vision camera in his lap, and they both kept their eyes and ears open for any ripples, splashes, or bubbles from where Rickie had made his previous appearance.

What they heard instead was a vehicle approaching the distant shore. It looked like a delivery truck. Amanda stared, but in the fading light she could not make out the writing on the side. The box truck backed right up to the water on the opposite side of the lake.

Then, while Vincent and Amanda watched in horror, two men jumped out of the vehicle, opened the back doors, and rolled massive barrels to the edge of the lake. They used crowbars to pry the barrels' lids off and then overturned them, pouring their contents directly into the water!

"Vincent, quick!" Amanda hissed, grabbing Vincent's arm. "Record this using your night-vision camera. We've got to get evidence. We can't allow this to stand!"

The truck driver and his partner dumped barrel after barrel into the water, causing the lake to bubble like a witch's cauldron. When they finished emptying the barrels, they started hurling junk into the water, too— giant chunks of who-knows-what. Amanda felt her face grow hot.

Amanda covered her mouth in dismay. These jerks were making Rickie's home even more toxic than it already was! There was no way they didn't know about the town's new cryptozoological mascot. He was in the national news. She couldn't allow this to continue. Even if there hadn't been a living being in this lake, whatever these creeps were doing was an environmental nightmare.

As soon as she took off her backpack, Amanda felt her antennae sprout from her head. Her marvelous exoskeletal armor hardened into place. Her wings unfurled and flapped so fast they were barely visible as she hovered, her hands clenched in fists. She was Bug Girl! And she was ready.

"Yeah, Bug Girl!" Vincent cheered. "Go kick their butts!"

"Not yet. These two are only part of the problem. I'm going to follow them back to their base. When I've taken care of their boss, we'll make sure these creeps never dump another thing anywhere except in prison! Vincent, record everything that happens and call the police as soon as they take off."

"Aye aye, captain!" Vincent saluted. He positioned himself in front of his camera and zoomed in on the action, making sure to get clear images of the truck's license plate and the offenders' faces.

Bug Girl soared high over the lake, keeping her distance so the creeps wouldn't spot her. If they took off running into the tangled nightmare of wires, crates, runoff tunnels, and garbage that lined the shores of Rickets, she might never find them.

The two toadies finished their terrible task and got back into the truck's cab. When the engine revved, a giant black cloud of exhaust shot out the back.

"Naturally," Bug Girl sighed. These people didn't care about the planet at all.

The truck groaned and growled as it crunched its way over years of rubbish along the shore, climbing back onto the asphalt that led away from Rickets Lake. Through the deserted parking lot of the Shoppes at South Clam it lumbered. Bug Girl hung back.

The nondescript truck wound its way through town until it finally reached a seedy warehouse on the outskirts. GREASY GARY'S CARPET AND PAINT, the sign read. Bug Girl

recognized the name from cheesy commercials on TV. "We'll carpet anything!" Greasy Gary shouted from the screen. She hated those commercials. Taking this turkey down was going to be satisfying!

The warehouse was a dump. Workers on forklifts lazily moved pallets of wall-and-floor-covering materials as the delivery truck pulled inside.

When Bug Girl saw the workers pull into the warehouse, jump out of the cab, and walk into an office, she flew into action. She raced right past the stunned forklift drivers and burst through the door.

"This is a bust!" she shouted. Greasy Gary jumped up from behind a filthy oaken desk, and the driver and his accomplice scuttled like rats to cower behind him. Bug Girl flapped her wings, her hands on her hips. "You people have dumped your last load of waste into Rickets Lake, and now you're going to pay for what you've done!"

Greasy Gary scoffed. "Ain't no kid gonna tell me what I'm gonna do," he grunted. "You know how much it costs to get rid of toxic waste the legal way? More than I'm willing to pay, I'll tell you that much. That lake's so filthy it doesn't matter what goes in it."

"I'm no 'kid.' I'm Bug Girl. And I stand for justice—environmental and otherwise. You messed with the wrong body of water, and I've got the proof that's going to lock you away and shut your business down forever!"

Greasy Gary looked at Bug Girl. He looked at the door behind her. Then he turned and ran. In her haste, Bug Girl hadn't noticed that the office had a back exit.

"Why, I oughtta . . ." Greasy Gary wheezed. He pushed past his workers and raced through the back door into the night air. Bug Girl decided not to waste her time on the two toadies and hightailed it after the real perp.

Greasy Gary was *not* getting away. Not a chance. Bug Girl sent Vincent a text telling him exactly where to send the police. She told him to get his video evidence downtown right away. Then she zipped up into the sky and looked down at the criminal carpet king trying desperately to find a place to hide.

She swooped down, considering Greasy Gary's punishment as she closed in. When she was close, she felt a stirring in her gut and intuitively unleashed a spray from her fingers. The liquid struck the fleeing fiend, and he stopped dead in his tracks, unable to move.

"Allomones!" she wondered out loud, gazing at her fingertips. A new power had just revealed itself. It looked just like a splatter of fruit juice—but it was actually a chemical bath that entered Greasy Gary's body and temporarily froze his muscles. He was still awake—he just couldn't move. The chemical concoction she'd unleashed was used by lacewings and other bugs to paralyze prey or would-be attackers. The insect kingdom never ceased to amaze!

Bug Girl rubbed her fingertips together and stood up a little taller. She could hear sirens coming in the distance and she had the polluting poltroon right where she wanted him.

When the police arrived, Bug Girl handed Greasy Gary over, explaining exactly what he had been doing. The lazy litterer, who was just getting his movement back as the allomones' effect wore off, admitted everything as tears streamed down his face.

"But it's just so expensive," he sobbed as he was crammed into the back of the police car.

Bug Girl shook her head at the cheap jerk. Didn't he know that there was a far heavier price to pay for spoiling the environment? Some people.

She lifted off and headed for home. If she hurried, she would still be able to finish her homework before bed.

BEADED LACEWING

Fun Bug Fact: Baby beaded lacewings live inside termite nests. When they get hungry, they release allomones that stun the much larger termites, paralyzing them. Then the lacewings eat the termites alive!

9

Satisfied with a job well done, Amanda spent the rest of her evening completing her English assignment and pondering ways to salvage Rickets Lake. It couldn't be completely beyond redemption, could it? The samples Sh'Shelle had taken would yield some valuable information, and the Entomological Society could act once they'd analyzed them. But that didn't stop Amanda's mind from wandering. She pictured a massive project involving teams of world-renowned scientists, the very tops of their respective fields, working together to bring this body of water back from the brink of doom. Their experiments, discoveries, and environmental cleanup technology would work wonders, and the lake would be saved!

When Amanda arrived at school the next day, the hot topic in the hallways was, of course, Bug Girl's most recent adventure. Greasy Gary's downfall had made the morning news. Bug Girl was once again being hailed as a hero. Not only had she saved the town from a major litterer but also from the most annoying ad campaign to air on TV in decades! Even though Amanda could not publicly take credit for Bug Girl's victory, she enjoyed listening to the chatter.

Unfortunately Bug Girl fans were not the only thing she had to listen to at school. She also needed to pay attention to Mr. Schenkenclabber's lecture on planarians—old news to a girl who had been studying bugs since preschool.

Amanda tried to look perky while the science teacher excitedly discussed the fact that if a planarian was cut in two, it could grow into TWO planarians! "Imagine how amazing it would be," Mr. Schenkenclabber wheezed, "if you were able to regenerate like that! Imagine the possibilities!"

Amanda preferred not to imagine. If humans were able to regenerate, there could be armies of identical jerks wandering the streets. She squeezed her eyes shut, picturing an army of Geris and her identical followers. Horrors!

Amanda snuck a glance at Geri and Emily at their desks in the corner of the room. They were right where she knew they would be. Side by side. Thick as thieves. But around them were several empty seats. Sadie Bimmins and Lorricent Grandy were out again today, and now Mikki Folders was gone, too! How could it be possible that three of the trendy set would be out at the same time? Skipping school together would be too obvious, and the last thing these girls would ever want was a tarnished reputation. Either there was a nasty virus going around, or something funky was brewing.

"Vincent," Amanda whispered, leaning over to her right and trying to be as discreet as possible. "Have you noticed how many kids are out? It's weird. I mean, where's Mikki Folders? She never misses a day. She would ask to be wheeled into class in an iron lung before she'd get an absent mark!"

"Calypso wasn't in French class this morning, either!" Vincent said. "Something is *étrange*, that's for sure!" He paused. "But it's only the top-tier girls. . . . Think of how much more pleasant school life could be if this trend continues!"

The thought of a snob-free zone was very soothing.

But Amanda felt something sinister was afoot. Her insect sensors agreed, stirring slightly. She put her hands on top of her head and immediately thought of steaming bowls of gooey, delicious mac and cheese. School emergency or not, the last thing she needed was to pop her antennae in the middle of science class!

"I'm going to see Ms. DeMartino during lunch," Vincent said. Nikki DeMartino was the seventh graders' guidance counselor, and Vincent had once-weekly meetings with her to discuss his scholarship opportunities and college options. "I'll see if I can snatch the attendance sheets while I'm in the main office; perhaps that will shed some light on things."

"I'll wait for you in the hall," Amanda said, feeling hopeful. Even though every one of the absent students had been awful to her and basically everyone she was friends with, she couldn't sit by if something potentially dangerous was happening to them.

Mr. Schenkenclabber was in midsentence, still waxing on about planarians' regenerative abilities, when the bell rang. Students grossed out by the science teacher's lecture about microslugs happily gathered their books and scampered for the door.

Amanda and Vincent lingered to finalize their plan.

"I'm going to lunch. I'll be outside the main-office door in twenty minutes," Amanda told her friend before they left the classroom. "Oh, and Vincent, there's one more item I should probably mention."

She swallowed. Given how things had been going in school the past few days, what she was about to say wouldn't be popular. "If we think there's something going on after we look at those attendance sheets, I think we should talk to Emily."

Vincent pinched his face into a grimace but soon relaxed. "Fine." He sighed. "If she acts nasty, I'll just ask her if she got her knockoff outfit at the flea market or inquire about the brand of spray tan she uses. I've learned how to handle that one; don't you worry."

Amanda rarely worried about Vincent.

In the cafeteria, Amanda stopped in her tracks when she heard a familiar voice.

"This jiggly goo was never a fish," Geri shouted at Hoagie Joe through the little window between the kitchen and the cafeteria. She held up her "fishwich" and lifted the bun off. Strings of clear slime pulled away from the whitish loaf hiding underneath wilted lettuce and something orange that might have been cheese. "This can't be a natural substance. This is poisonous, and I refuse to eat it! I won't!"

"Go hungry. See if I care," came a growl through the window. Hoagie Joe then appeared, shoving his entire upper body out the kitchen window. He was covered in sauce and grease. He waved a coated spoon toward Geri, splashing gray glop on passing students. They screamed and ran, but that didn't faze Hoagie Joe one bit. "Tomorrow we're having bologna boats, so get ready," he yelled, scratching beneath his hairnet with the spoon.

"If I die from this food, I'm totally going to sue you," Geri shouted back. She stormed away, and Amanda watched her slam her tray down at the table where the popular girls generally sat. Three seats were empty.

Emily sashayed over and sat down next to Geri, smiling and chatting as if the two of them had been friends forever. As if she had known Geri since they were babies and had been through amazing adventures with her. Precisely the way Amanda wished Emily would talk to her.

A sliver of sadness lodged in Amanda's throat, making it hard to breathe. She swallowed until the pain went away and forced herself to refocus on the situation at hand.

Quickly she surveyed the other popular tables. On the other side of the cafeteria, the eighth graders' royal court was looking thinned-out as well. Dipsy Bevelfunken, the reigning queen of the upper class, was MIA, as were Koky Masterbland and Vivienne Fud. All popular, all gone. The grades generally kept to themselves and had their own klatches, cliques, and groups, but it was hard not to notice when the very, very top of the school's popular tier went missing.

Since school had only just begun, the sixth graders hadn't been able to fully label each student as "popular," "meh," or "untouchable" yet. They were still sorting out their self-imposed popularity ranking system. And Amanda didn't know many of them, so she was unsure if any had fallen prey to the absentee mystery.

She looked at the clock. It was already time to meet Vincent! She stuffed the containers Poppy had packed for her back into her lunch tote, waved to her crew, and scuttled away down the hall.

Vincent was waiting by the main office, as planned. He had the master attendance book in his lap, already open to the week's roster. Sadie and Lorricent, it turned out, had been absent since last Thursday . . . a full week! The eighth graders had all been absent since Monday. Adding Mikki to the list made one thing clear—popular girls were definitely going missing.

"Vincent, sneak back in there with this and put it where it belongs," Amanda instructed. "Then I want you to get on to the intercom system. Deepen your voice as much as possible and request that Emily Battfield come to the main office!"

Vincent looked like he might faint. Getting on the intercom was not something he had signed up for. But Amanda shot him a pleading look, letting him know that this was urgent business, and the pale boy walked back into the office.

Amanda waited outside and listened.

After a few misfires that sounded like the crackles of cheap fireworks going off, the school's intercom system came to life.

"Emily Battfield," the deep-enough voice croaked, "please, um, please report to the main office. Right now."

Vincent, looking depleted, rejoined Amanda in the hallway. "That was the worst moment of my life," he whined, clutching his chest dramatically. "Public speaking on that scale has never been one of my strong points. I feel like I may need to lie down for a moment."

"You did fabulously, as always," Amanda assured him. "You're a natural." He relaxed a bit and took a small bow.

The two heard Emily before they saw her. Her stomps echoed through the halls, creating a racket akin to a monster-truck rally. The steps pounded nearer.

Amanda swallowed hard.

Facing Emily in school was never fun.

PLANARIAN

Fun Fact: Planarians are flatworms that live in fresh or salt water. They have a special power: If they get cut into pieces, each piece regenerates into a brand-new planarian in just a few weeks!

10

"**I** should have known from that froglike voice that this was all a trick," Emily seethed when Amanda and Vincent intercepted her on the way to the office. "It's embarrassing enough to be called over the intercom—I mean, when does that EVER happen anymore?—but to risk being seen in the hall with half of the Crustacean Brigade or whatever you call yourselves . . . I'm simply mortified." She dropped her voice to a whisper and skewered Amanda with a look. "And how DARE you get more media play than me? I heard all about your little solo adventure last night!"

"What was I supposed to do—call you and wait to do anything until you showed up? I had to act fast," Amanda whisper-shouted back.

"Get to the point," Emily said impatiently.

Amanda clenched her teeth. Emily could really work

a nerve. "You're supposed to trust me. I trusted you. . . . That's what partners do. I wouldn't have asked Vincent to call you out of class if it wasn't important!"

Amanda took a deep breath and braced herself. She had to get through to her partner here and now. "Emily, listen to me. Haven't you noticed that your *friends* are missing? Sadie and Lorricent have been out since late last week! And today Mikki is gone!"

"Oh, please." Emily waved her hand dismissively. "You blurted my name over the school intercom for that? I have far more important things to focus on than truancy. For example, the theme for the dance was just announced. You probably weren't paying any attention. But, FYI, it's 'Disco Daze.'"

"Wait." Amanda held her hand up like a stop sign. "What? How is there a dance already? And how does that matter *at all*?"

Amanda and Vincent stared at Emily with dumbfounded expressions. They blinked.

"I mean, it's THE dance," Emily replied as if that were an answer. "The one that sets the tone for the entire

OCMS DISCO DAZE DANCE
Next Thursday
GET READY TO GET DOWN! VOTE FOR YOUR FAVORITE DANCING QUEEN!

school year." Emily grew wistful as she continued, locked in a reverie. "Every seventh grader in the history of Oyster Cove Middle School has coveted being the Dancing Queen—the person who presses the button that gets the disco ball spinning. This year, I will be the Dancing Queen. I'll turn on the disco ball and start the dance." She swayed gently back and forth, lost in the vision. "It's going to be the best!" Her expression soured. "Even if the ball is turning to 1970s throwback music and everyone just stands around awkwardly instead of actually dancing. . . ."

Amanda groaned. Of course Emily was more concerned about winning a popularity contest than solving what could potentially be a crime. Even if that crime involved her friends. If Amanda didn't know that Emily was actually a crime-fighting superhero, she would have bet that Emily was HAPPY her friends were missing. It meant there would be less competition to win the Dancing Queen nomination!

"Emily, for real—you need to focus on this," Amanda said. "The dance is not important. I need you to help me figure this out! Even Dipsy Bevelfunken is missing!"

Emily gasped.

Amanda thought she had finally gotten through to her partner. She thought Emily would leap into action and fight for justice.

But she was wrong.

Emily held her hands over her mouth and stared down

the hall. The look on her face was one of sheer horror. Amanda was almost afraid to look at whatever was causing Emily's expression! But slowly she turned.

The corridor was lined with posters—all professionally made from the looks of them. Glossy, shiny, glittering posters. Each featuring Geri in a different pose and outfit.

Geri is the Dancing Queen 4 U, one exclaimed in lettering suitable for ironing on a T-shirt with a photo of Geri in a red sequined jumpsuit. *Don't Be a Jive Turkey—Vote for Geri!* another screamed above a photo featuring Geri wearing patchwork flares, roller skates, and a puffy-sleeve satin blouse.

"How did she know?" Emily screamed, threatening to fracture the glass in the trophy case. "When did she have the time? This was just announced *today*! HOW?"

Emily fell to her knees and slammed her books down hard. She sobbed, and doors up and down the hallway popped open to see what was causing the ruckus.

"Um, Emily. It's a dance," Amanda offered, not really feeling very sympathetic. *Give me a break*, she thought to herself.

"I'm going to win," Emily said, regaining her focus and standing back up. Brushing herself off and adjusting her hair, she seethed, "I was queen of this school before Geri arrived, and I am queen of this school now. I'm going to beat Geri. I will be the Dancing Queen of Oyster Cove Middle School!"

Amanda and Vincent exchanged knowing, disgusted glances. But the pair was invisible to Emily, who was now pacing and making mental lists.

"I'm going to have to hire the best public relations team," Emily mumbled. "And find a local company that can print buttons. And maybe balloons. And I should hire an image consultant to help with power outfits. And I need to do it all before next Thursday!"

"Perhaps between sessions with the consultant you haven't hired yet, you might want to focus on the fact that at least six students are mysteriously absent?" Amanda asked but to no avail. Emily's mind had left the conversation a long time ago. Amanda knew one thing for sure—if Emily thought there was a chance she'd come in second place in a popularity contest, she would stop at nothing to achieve first.

Emily collected her books and stomped down the hall. All Amanda could do was watch. Her shoulders slumped.

"That went well," Vincent joked.

11

Emily pulled her chunky knit sweater over her head, tossed it on a growing pile of rejected outfits, and slammed her foot in frustration. The resulting tremor set off car alarms around the neighborhood—and that was just from Emily feeling peevish. When the shaking subsided, Emily stood silently in a sea of cast-off garments. She listened for Frida's footsteps on the stairs, expecting an earful about controlling her temper (and powers), but nobody came. *Good*, Emily thought. She was in no mood for Frida's lessons today. She was feeling completely out of sorts, and it was seriously hampering her ability to coordinate an outfit. Since when, if ever, did *Emily Battfield* have trouble putting together an outfit?

Since I started being super, Emily thought. It was, to say the least, both ironic and a total bummer that at the same time she became aware of her destiny as a hero, she also began, for the first time, to experience self-doubt. She'd even started having trouble making decisions. *But we're talking clothes here, not a superhero name!* Emily clenched her fists to keep herself from stomping again. It made sense that choosing a supername—something that would stay with you for your whole career—would be difficult. It was a moniker she'd have to live with forever; it would go down in history! At least, it was supposed to. "And not as a laughingstock," Emily mumbled to herself.

She couldn't admit it publicly—she could barely admit it to herself—but training alongside Bug Girl was the thing filling her with doubt. It made no sense that Amanda had better powers than she did. The girl could *fly*! And she could hock disintegration loogies! Okay, well, *that* was gross. But still. And Emily, after months of relentless training, had only developed a power scream, a seismic stomp, and a shiny outfit? It just wasn't enough.

Seriously, it chapped her hide that Amanda was just . . . better. At everything. Bug Girl could jump, lift, solve, blast, liquefy . . .

Before all of these *super*developments, Emily was the

one who did things first, right, and best. For example, when they took gymnastics, Emily had mastered cartwheels, back handsprings, and perfect round-offs, while Amanda could only get one foot off the ground at a time! But that was before Ms. Genius grew wings.

Emily had hoped that being back in school and getting some time away from Amanda—to protect their identities—would help her feel more like herself again. She'd even found the perfect new cohort in Geri, the transfer student.

Emily admired Geri straightaway—she had flawless style, high school–level smarts, a discerning worldview, and commanding panache, plus she was practically fearless. Just like Emily used to be. It was probably the first time Emily had met another girl who measured up to her own caliber of social supremacy. They bonded instantly, and Emily even thought that Geri had the potential to elevate Emily's already towering social stature. They were practically inseparable.

Although, they never *really* talked.

Emily gazed up at her ceiling. She thought back, trying

to count in her head how many words she and Geri had actually spoken to each other. It was definitely fewer than one hundred. Mostly they just looked at each other and exchanged knowing glances, or eye-rolls, or raised their eyebrows in unison.

But now, with the dance . . .

The dance changed everything. Emily would have happily ruled the school with Geri. But Geri wasn't with her. She probably never had been. Geri was against her. And taking her down would require nothing less than social genius.

First off, Emily could not appear to angrily oppose Geri, so competing against her for the title of Dancing Queen was going to be sticky business. She would have to tread carefully so as not to incur Geri's wrath.

Emily picked up her discarded sweater and put it back on. She looked in the mirror and considered her next move. It might be smart to simply concede, since Geri already had the jump on her in campaigning. Emily could maintain some status that way, by making it look like it was her idea to let the new girl win. But Dancing Queen was not a title Emily was willing to give up. It was an opportunity she'd been anticipating forever. Just the idea of someone else being awarded *her* title was horrifying. And to lose to a girl who hadn't even been at the school a full year? No. Emily had to win.

The school's social arena was the one area of Emily's life where she felt she had control. She could not lose there. Nor could she yield. She *might* have shared once but not anymore.

Emily tore off the sweater once more. She picked up a striped shirt from her heap of rejected clothes. She pulled it on and checked her reflection. *Not bad.* She added a black skirt. A denim jacket. Bangles. *Better.* Tucking her hair behind her ears and slipping on her favorite kicks, Emily felt her confidence slowly returning. She had not lost her touch.

Then it suddenly occurred to Emily how she could defeat Geri. Though she admired many aspects of Geri's snappy personality, there was one key difference between them: Geri treated the socially awkward with disdain—the entire seventh grade tried to hide from her to avoid fashion tickets and public humiliation—while Emily had heretofore simply ignored the lower ranks. *But perhaps . . .*

Emily added a scarf to her ensemble and then quickly rejected it. She already looked perfect.

It was important not to go too far or to take the fear that Geri instilled in her classmates lightly. Students might be afraid *not* to vote for Geri. It was a sick loyalty. But there it was.

Emily considered the chorus of girls she surrounded herself with. Those girls' social orbits included Geri now, too. But she still had them in her pocket, didn't she? Hadn't Amanda called them Emily's "friends"? Unfortunately Amanda had also pointed out that they were all truants who were "out sick."

"Or hiding under their beds, afraid of getting a fashion ticket," Emily muttered under her breath. It was a problem . . . but one she was sure Amanda would handle in the same way she handled everything else. After all, Amanda was the one with all the powers . . . at least outside of school.

Emily kicked a path to her door. "Those little *mademoiselles* had better start showing up," she grumbled, grabbing the sheaf of campaign posters she'd made.

She had a title to win.

And she was going to need their votes.

12

Saturday dawned way too bright and way too early for Emily's liking. She had barely removed her sleeping mask when the front-door chimes announced the arrival of Amanda and Poppy. Annoyingly punctual, as always.

After hanging up dozens of posters, passing out hundreds of buttons, and reassuring Geri with a fake smile that she was sure to win and that the only reason she, Emily, didn't drop out of the competition was that her mom would have been way too sad—which causes stress wrinkles—on Friday, Emily was exhausted. And now she had to do weekend superhero training. Barf. Since when did her life require so much . . . effort?

While Frida let Amanda and Poppy in, Emily pulled on some spandex warm-up clothes, did a couple of yoga stretches, and pondered the downturn of her life. At the end of the last school year, when she and Amanda had

SURYA NAMASKAR A

A yoga warm-up*

1   2   3   4   5   6

7   8   9   10   11

*Don't do it alone unless you're experienced!

their little adventure, saved their mothers, and discovered their true natures, Emily had to admit—she'd been excited.

It was really no shock that she was the daughter of Megawoman. Duh. That made perfect sense. But what made less sense was the lag in her development. Where were her megapowers? Why hadn't she radically transformed already?

Emily sighed and gave up on her downward-facing dog pose. She tried some cat and cow poses instead. Not being the best at being super made her feel like . . . a loser.

It was one thing when she had to deal with that privately, on weekends, and during training, but now, with the dance debacle, the icky feelings were seriously encroaching on school turf, which made her feel like a double loser.

Emily rolled up her glittery yoga mat and stormed down the hall to the kitchen. Amanda was sitting at the huge marble island, eating one of Frida's Morning Glorious Muffins. Poppy and Frida were nowhere to be seen.

"Good morning!" Amanda chirped. Her cheeks were pink. Her eyes were wide. Her enthusiasm completely squashed Emily's appetite. "Poppy said that today we should probably work on triangulation attacks so we can decrease collateral damage and spare innocents," Amanda burbled. She took another muffin.

Emily took one, too. She didn't want to eat it; she just didn't want Amanda to have them all.

"And speaking of innocents," Amanda went on, "we really need to talk about the school situation. Geri's fashion-police shtick is out of control. It's causing a tissue short-age in the restrooms, because so many students are hiding there to cry. Her couture tyranny has got to stop!"

Honestly, Emily agreed. Geri was taking things too far. But she wasn't about to admit that to Amanda. She'd never hear the end of it.

"Maybe if people put a little effort into their wardrobes, they wouldn't be so scared," Emily said. She stuffed a bit of muffin in her mouth and chewed slowly.

Amanda stopped chewing. She turned red. "Are you kidding? Do you even know what it's like to be humiliated publicly?" she demanded. "Do you have any idea?"

Emily had never been picked on in her life. But she imagined it felt a little like being shown up at every turn by someone you used to call a friend. It was an awful feeling, but what was *she* supposed to do about it? She couldn't spend every waking moment protecting the feelings of OCMS students. Helping didn't come as naturally to her as it did to Amanda. Why, that girl was *always* looking out for others . . . even tadpoles. What was that frog of hers named? *Clover? Clytemnestra? Cletus?* Whatever it was, Emily remembered walking up to Amanda while she was giving that baby frog a pep talk last year in science. Amanda cared about *everything*.

"Have you even noticed the redheaded kids becoming goths and emos?" Amanda went on angrily. "Geri's so mean to them that they're all dressing like they're going to a funeral. And the rest of the student body is going to follow pretty quickly if we don't do something about it!"

" 'We'?" Emily fixed Amanda with a look. "Why don't *you* do something about it? You seem able to fix everything else. . . ."

"Emily, I need your help to stop Geri!" Amanda pleaded. She looked at Emily with round eyes. Her voice got softer. "She's your friend. Maybe she just needs help. My mom always says that mean behavior stems from some deeper hurt. Maybe Geri's like a wounded animal lashing out."

Emily turned away. Her stomach churned. Leave it to Amanda to feel bad for Geri. Emily tried to imagine the new mean queen as a helpless tadpole swirling in a bowl. She tried to feel bad for her. She tried to stop feeling bad for herself. But there was simply no way she could weaken herself in Geri's eyes by trying to convince her to act nice or by suggesting that she was lashing out because she was hurt.

No. This was Amanda's gig.

Emily turned back around. She leaned in close. "Look: I'm not the boss of her," she said in measured tones. "If *you* don't like what Geri's doing, you should do something about it."

Amanda gaped like a goldfish. Her mouth opened and closed, but for several long seconds, nothing came out. "But . . . we're partners," she finally said.

"Don't be silly. You can do it alone," Emily replied. "You're *Bug Girl*, aren't you?"

13

A manda felt the presence of the bad guy before she saw him. Trusting her instincts, she spun quickly and aimed the heel of her boot where she knew his chest would be. Only, it wasn't there. She connected with air, lost her balance, and had to use her wings to keep from face-planting next to the villain decoy she'd been targeting. It wasn't pretty.

"Oops. Sorry." Emily was standing in the spot where the target had been. She knew Amanda was going after it, had pushed it over—on purpose—and was now watching Amanda flail to stay upright with an expression on her face that certainly wasn't "sorry."

Once she'd regained her footing, Amanda ground her teeth together and shot Emily a look. What was she doing? They were *supposed* to be on the same side. Now it felt like Emily was actively working against her!

Amanda dusted herself off and wished, not for the first time, that she could have chosen her own partner. She would have much rather paired up with Vincent, even if he didn't have any powers! Frankly, she would have preferred pretty much anyone else. Trying to make Emily work with her was, well, not working.

"Tell Poppy I'm walking home." Amanda pulled off her Bug Girl mask and headed toward the Airstream in front of the Battfields' house.

"What, you can't handle the unexpected?" Emily asked innocently. "I'm only trying to help you hone your powers!"

Amanda turned and glared. Who was Emily kidding? She was sabotaging her! "Hone your own powers!" Amanda grumbled.

Emily sucked in her breath. She looked like she had more to say, but Amanda wasn't waiting around to hear it.

Poppy and Frida had left strict instructions for the girls to do seventeen Lunges Around the World reps *before* they started their exercises, but they had not stayed to monitor their progress.

They'd been doing that a lot lately—disappearing as soon as they'd given the girls their assignments. Amanda assumed they were trading recipes for casseroles and explosives.

"Am I the only one who cares . . . about anything?" Amanda shouted at the empty trailer.

It was a long walk from Langoustine Estates back to Amanda's neighborhood, and Amanda chose the extra-extra-long route so she could walk past Rickets Lake. She needed to calm down, and Rickie had been on her mind ever since the Greasy Gary bust. The dumping had stopped, but she was still worried about his survival in that beleaguered bog. It needed cleaning. The creature hadn't been spotted since he'd surfaced for the Entomological Society. Amanda suspected the crowds were frightening him, but she couldn't rule out something worse.

She heard the horde of noisy tourists long before she could see the water. The crowd was thicker than ever . . . and more obnoxious. Emboldened by their numbers, they had erected ramshackle campsites on any scrap of land they could find. There, perched on chairs and ladders and makeshift scaffolds, they kept their cameras pointed at Rickie's puddle while littering what was left of the landscape with food wrappers and general waste.

"You dropped this," Amanda said pointedly, picking up a bladder-busting-size drink cup and putting it back into the hand of the oblivious litterer who'd tossed it to the ground. The man looked at her blankly and dropped the disposable cup again. "Don't worry; I'll get it," Amanda said. Without cracking a smile or breaking eye contact, she retrieved the cup again and carried it to a trash bin. Perhaps he could learn from her example.

Amanda took a bag from her backpack and began collecting more trash as she made her way to the water's edge. When she got there, she sucked in her breath and immediately regretted it. The stench made her gag. Though she wouldn't have thought it possible, the water in the lake was worse than last time! *There's a word for that color*, she thought. . . . *Puce*. It was a word that described a flea in French and also the muddy purple color of flea droppings. It was hardly something you would want to swim in.

"I hope you're okay out there," Amanda whispered

softly toward the center of the lake as she fished a Nougat Nosh wrapper out of the muck. "I'll think of some way to clean this up. I promise."

Amanda stood staring at the water for a long time. Before leaving, she squatted down and sprinkled a few more Cricket Crispies on the damp ground. Amphibians loved those treats. She closed her eyes and pictured her sweet tadpole Cletus gobbling the amphibian treats like a gourmet dinner—and she hoped that Rickie would enjoy the snack, too. She didn't want anyone watching to think that she was littering, but if Rickie was still alive, she needed to give the critter a fighting chance.

On Sunday, Amanda was up before the sun. She liked to get up early because many of the bugs she kept in her room were more active during the dim hours than in daylight. She talked to her multi-legged pets softly as she cleaned their cages and made sure they had fresh food and water.

Trina crawled onto Amanda's arm as she worked, and Amanda paused to stroke the roach's glossy shell with her fingertip.

As soon as it was light enough, Amanda called Vincent. He was also an early riser, even on Sundays, so she knew she wouldn't wake him.

"Good morning!" Vincent chirped into the phone.

"Good morning," Amanda said quickly. Then she got down to business. "Vincent, can you access school records from home?"

There was a brief silence before Vincent replied, "Weeelll, not *officially*."

Amanda knew what that meant: *yes!* "Perfect!" she said, grinning. "We need the addresses of all the girls who have been absent over the last two weeks! You and I are going to be making some house calls to see what's up with these so-called sickies."

This time the silence on the other end of the line lasted a bit longer.

"I can get you the addresses, Amanda. But . . . I'm afraid I have other plans for today. So you'll have to make those house calls on your own."

Amanda felt her enthusiasm deflate just a little bit. She had been looking forward to spending time with Vincent.

The two of them worked so well together, they always had a good time, and lately they'd both been so busy. . . . It felt like everyone was abandoning her. But Vincent's sheepish tone let her know that he was bummed out, too. Whatever it was that was taking up Vincent's time must've been important—unlike Emily's excuses.

"I understand," she said, trying to keep the disappointment out of her voice. "You do what you need to, and I'll give you a full report by this evening."

"I shall look forward to it," Vincent replied.

Less than an hour later, Amanda arrived at her first stop. She looked at the printout in her hand and matched it to the address of the house before her: 42 Bivalvia Lane. If anyone had suggested to Amanda three months ago that she would be approaching the home of Mikki Folders *willingly*, she would have guffawed. Other than tripping her at Emily's birthday party (and sending her headlong into the punch), Mikki had a nasty habit of snickering like a hissy snake behind her hand whenever Amanda passed her in the hallway. It was beyond rude.

Yet here she was.

Amanda strode up the walkway with as much confidence as she could muster. She was wearing a blazer and cap she had borrowed from Poppy in an attempt to look "official." On her lapel she had a homemade badge. And in her hands was a clipboard—the ultimate prop for reinforcing legitimacy. The overall effect was fairly convincing—so long as nobody noticed her age.

Mr. Folders opened the door wearing a bathrobe and slippers. Mrs. Folders appeared behind him a moment later, carrying a coffee cup and a very small dog . . . or a very large rat. "Can I help you?" Mr. Folders asked.

Amanda cleared her throat. "Good morning. I am Officer Hydrangea from the Oyster Cove Truancy Agency. I'm conducting an inquiry into the recent absence of your daughter, Mikki Folders, from school."

Mr. Folders blinked. Mrs. Folders blinked. The rat dog took a slurp of Mrs. Folders's coffee.

"Mikki?" Mr. Folders asked.

"Yes. Your daughter," Amanda repeated in case he was confused.

"I know who my daughter is!" Mr. Folders replied, sounding a little irritated. "It's Sunday, young lady. And you say you're from the school?"

Amanda was about to repeat that she was from the Truancy Agency when Mrs. Folders jumped in.

"Of course Mikki has been absent from school," she said, shouldering her way past her husband. "Our Mikki was invited to a special camp! For *smart* kids."

Now it was Amanda's turn to blink. Mikki? Smart?

"I've got the letter right here!" Mrs. Folders shuffled into the kitchen with Mr. Folders and Amanda right behind her. She put the dog and the cup on the counter and rooted around in a stack of papers before shoving one in Amanda's face.

Oyster Cove Middle School
2 Tiny Hillock Drive
Oyster Cove

Dear Parents,
Congratulations! Your child has been selected to attend the world-renowned Obfuscation and Verbosity Debate Camp. This honor is granted to those gifted in

the argumentative arts. We were especially impressed by your child's ranting abilities and wailing techniques, and we look forward to welcoming her into our debate community.

The official OVDC bus will transport your child to the camp on opening day. We eagerly await her arrival.

Sincerely,
Hazel Hedgebottom

Amanda read the letter over twice, trying to make sense of it. Yes, the school's address was on the top. Yes, it sounded official. Yes, Mikki could wail. But who would eagerly await her arrival for anything at all and *why*?

The Folders stared at Amanda intensely while she made tutting noises, shook her head, and wrote things down on her clipboard. "Slipped through the cracks," she mumbled. "Poor communication." She hoped her muffled words were soothing, as she really didn't want to alarm Mikki's parents—not until she got to the bottom of this.

"So Mikki was picked up in a bus?" she asked, not making eye contact. It was tough to ask questions without triggering suspicion.

Mrs. Folders nodded. "Yes. It was a strange bus. But it arrived the morning after we got the letter."

Mr. Folders nodded, too, and licked his lips. "I liked that bus," he said wistfully. "It made me crave French fries."

"Very good. Very good." Amanda kept her head down and her cap covering her eyes as she backed out of the Folders' home. "I'm sure Mikki is having a fine time arguing with the best of them," she concluded. "Sorry for the interruption."

The door clicked shut behind her as she left. Amanda pedaled her bicycle to the next house as quickly as she could.

When she reached the Grandy home, she removed her TRUANCY OFFICER badge and pursued a different tactic. After confirming that Lorricent had also been "selected" to attend debate camp, Amanda pretended to be conducting a survey for Obfuscation and Verbosity's marketing team.

"On a scale of one to ten, how happy were you with the notification of acceptance?" she asked, tapping her pencil on her clipboard.

"Oh, ten! Ten! We were over the moon!" the Grandys

clucked proudly over Lorricent's acceptance to camp—though neither could remember her applying. They were delighted that their little bonbon had been recognized for her remarkable long-windedness. They had always found it extraordinary themselves. Still, they could not believe their good fortune, nor could they fathom the quiet days and nights—they had been afraid to ask how many—they'd have away from their loquacious child. It truly was a dream come true.

"And how would you rate the camp transportation services?" Amanda asked.

Mrs. Grandy wrinkled her nose. "It smelled a little . . . greasy, but it arrived on time. I give it a seven on a scale of one to ten."

"And the driver?" Amanda pushed.

"Hmmm." Mr. Grandy put his hand to his chin. "Don't think I ever saw the driver. We just loaded in Lorricent's bags and they were off."

"Like a shot," Mrs. Grandy added with a sigh and a sweet smile.

After surveying more families, Amanda started for

home. There were things she knew, and things she didn't. One thing was certain: none of these girls had been recruited for their intelligence. She'd known three of them since they'd sat in circles together in preschool, and while they were all undeniably popular, they were also irrefutably dim. Strictly *C*-level. They had not been recruited. . . . They had been kidnapped! But who in their right minds would want to kidnap *them*?

FLEA

droppings

Fun Bug Fact: Puce comes from *puce*, the French word for *flea*. In English, it describes a purplish-brown hue, the color of fleas and their bloodstained droppings.

14

Amanda was over it. Officially. She had to get to the bottom of these sinister goings-on before the entire student body was reported missing, and she had to do it right now. The smelly, ramshackle bus was a definite clue, but she needed something more. Luckily, she knew just where to start looking.

She stormed into her modest home and tossed her backpack down on the couch. Poppy—who was apparently practicing an interpretive dance in the living room—pirouetted toward her.

"Hold up there, Mandy! Emily told us you didn't complete your training yesterday."

Amanda stopped in her tracks but didn't turn to look at Poppy, who, from the sound of it, was now doing a soft-shoe. "Did Emily also tell you that she is refusing to help me figure out why so many students have been absent from school? Did she tell you that all she cares about is being Dancing Queen and that stupid disco ball? Did she tell you that?"

The shuffling noises stopped. Poppy put his hand on Amanda's shoulder.

"You can't just go running away every time you two get into an argy-bargy," Poppy wheezed. "Kerfuffles have to be worked out, or you'll never be a good team."

"You're right, Poppy," Amanda said, shrugging off his hand and stomping away. "We'll never be a good team."

Amanda was tired of thinking about Emily. And she was tired of questions. She wanted answers.

She clomped down the basement stairs and stepped onto her mother's treadmill, Zephyr. The exercise machine was the key to gaining access to her mother's secret lair. When set to level thirteen for a three-minute run, the contraption opened a secret door that led down, down, down to her mother's high-tech hideaway.

"She can't think of anyone besides herself," Amanda kept muttering. "Her friends are missing, and she's making posters and trying on accessories." She set the treadmill to

"Olympian Goddess"—the thirteenth and highest level—and began to run. She tried to push thoughts of Emily out of her mind as she picked up speed. Being mad would only distract her from her mission. She needed to concentrate! The popular set, even though they were totally snippy, needed her help.

After three minutes, the door to her mother's superhero base finally opened with a prolonged creak. Amanda jumped off Zephyr and stepped into the darkness.

"Welcome, Bug Girl!" a computerized voice burbled as she initiated the proper security scan. Her mother had granted her computer access after Bug Girl rescued her from The Exterminator. Dragonfly couldn't be sure that she would never be captured or incapacitated again, and she wanted her daughter to have all the tools necessary to battle crime on her own.

At the moment, however, Amanda wished her mother hadn't just up and vanished to her superhero spa week or expo or whatever it was. Her mom was an expert at dealing with these things, and frankly, although Bug Girl had proven she was a total and complete (plus amazing, if she did say so herself) hero, she could still use a little help.

She stared down at the keyboard. Where to start? She looked around the chamber at her mother's newspaper clippings, files, and keepsakes. There were so many dangers in the world, so many agents of malice. . . . Anybody could be a villain! And then she remembered why she had come down there in the first place—her mother's secret weapon against fiends: the Database of Evil.

Dragonfly and Megawoman had created the information bank years ago, which allowed other heroes around the globe to create, access, and update villain profiles. This helped them keep up to date on the world's various ne'er-do-wells, creeps, brigands, monsters, malevolent turkeys, and villains.

Amanda cracked her knuckles. She used the login her mother had created for her: *BugGirlKixButt.* She grimaced as she typed it in, but Amanda knew her mother thought it was funny.

The screen glowed black and green. As Amanda scrolled through the listings, she noticed something. While each scoundrel had his or her own entry, it appeared that they all maintained a sort of villain network.

For example, Dr. Mittens was a miscreant who would steal children's winter gear in Woonsocket, Rhode Island, leaving them forlorn and frostbitten. Standby Sasha, a scoundrel who would linger in airports and distract people long enough to make sure they missed their flights, called Townville, South Carolina, her home base. Yet the two of them had been sighted together in Buttonwillow, California, working with yet another character named Finicky LaRue, whose personal brand of badness was causing scenes in grocery stores over produce he perceived to be less than fresh. Once the entire staff was occupied with handling his complaints, Finicky's henchmen would rush into the store and rob it blind.

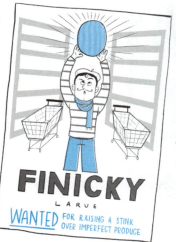

As Amanda kept scrolling, she saw that most of these baddies had teamed up with multiple partners on various forays into crime and mayhem. She was amazed! It seemed like they all knew one another and worked together to spread a blanket of discord across the land. This realization made Amanda a little queasy. If they were all talking to one another, they could be just as organized and prepared as the Global Hero Network was! It was a terrifying thought that did nothing to help figure out what was going on right here in Oyster Cove. Amanda shook her head and blinked her eyes. She needed to concentrate.

Kidnapping. Popular. Buses. Amanda searched some terms, but they resulted in a list of nine thousand entries! Then she added *Oyster Cove.*

Entry number one was someone named Coagula. She had been one of the hot villains in Oyster Cove in the late 1950s, way before Dragonfly's time. Coagula was famous for sneaking into soda shops where the youngsters gathered. She enjoyed using her Coagulation Ray to turn root beer solid, so the sock-hopping teenyboppers couldn't enjoy their floats, before cackling and disappearing into the night. According to the entry, she was no longer active.

"Some of these villains sure have strange hang-ups," Amanda mumbled. "I mean, who solidifies root beer?"

The next entry looked serious.

Synisteria was by all appearances a lovely woman, born and raised in Oyster Cove. Her evil turn came one afternoon when she saw a rerun of *The Shrieking Ghost of Pinebottom Swamp* at WTOC's Saturday afternoon Creature Feature Show.

According to the file, Synisteria's mother had been an avid monster-movie fan who dragged her daughter to every horror show that played at the local theater, regardless of the ratings. The poor girl had been terrified. She begged her mother to stop taking her, to which her mother responded, "Quit your whining. These movies build character."

The fear that those movies instilled in young Synisteria gave her awful insomnia. She lost so much sleep that she failed her cheerleading tryouts and had to endure the taunts and jeers of the squad. Synisteria was devastated— and deeply scarred.

For years the damaged girl was able to suppress the terror those films inflicted on her . . . until she stumbled upon that afternoon feature. Seeing it triggered something, and she snapped.

From that moment on, Synisteria was driven to inflict her horror movie–induced dementia upon unsuspecting, popular teens. She lured them to her home with promises of snacks and then forced them to watch scary movies over and over again.

During her active years, she subjected countless children to films such as *Don't Look in the Cookie Jar* and *The Legend of Cabin 12* in her modest Oyster Cove bungalow. She kept them for days, weeks, or sometimes

years before shooing them out the door and into the scary, dark night.

The horror maven was finally arrested when little Babette Drexelbolten, the head cheerleader at Oyster Cove Middle School, turned out to be immune to her methods. Synisteria had enticed Babette by promising to help perfect her triple-double backflip roundabout but had quickly turned on the TV and initiated her horror film treatment. But Babette, it turned out, actually LOVED monster movies.

After a seven-hour marathon of films like *Demon Kittens of the Old Northeast* and *Mr. Grodo Strikes Back*, Synisteria had seen no change in Babette's demeanor. The girl

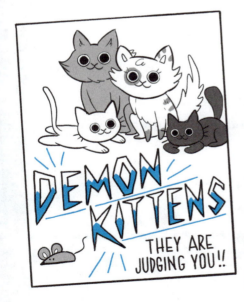

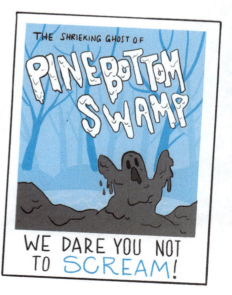

laughed and clapped and cheered. She'd even executed a triple back handspring.

Her evil spirit broken, Synisteria tried to kick Babette out, but Babette refused to leave. The perky girl asked to watch another movie. Synisteria couldn't take the child's enthusiasm. Defeated, she called Babette's parents and asked them to come pick their child up—and alert the authorities. She turned herself in.

"This lady's nuts!" Amanda said to the computer. She scrolled to the bottom to see her last-known whereabouts.

Synisteria, it turned out, had recently been released from Picklegraph Penitentiary and had returned to Oyster Cove! Under a work release program, she had changed her name to Ginny Lou Johnson and was employed at the Abel Goatslam Memorial Branch Library.

"Eureka!" Amanda shouted. A washed-up kidnapper back in Oyster Cove. It was a promising lead. And if Synisteria was up to her old tricks, Bug Girl would get to the bottom of it!

She picked up the phone and called Vincent, hoping he was through with his previous engagement.

When Vincent answered the phone, he was out of breath.

"Are you okay?" Amanda asked, concerned.

"Oh, sure, I'm, um, fine . . ." Vincent wheezed tentatively, as if searching for something to fill in the blanks. "I was just, uh, helping my mother carry in the groceries. And you know how that goes."

Amanda told Vincent all about Synisteria and what she had uncovered in her search.

"Sounds like a winner to me," Vincent said, finally regaining his composure. "What's the plan?"

"I was thinking we should go over to her house," Amanda said. It was pretty straightforward. If this horror hack was kidnapping popular girls and forcing them into scary movie marathons in her basement, her house would be the best place to start. "But we have to find it, which means we have to find her. Luckily we know that she now works at the library."

"Wait!" Vincent yelled, sounding excited. "We're going on a field trip to the Abel Goatslam Memorial Branch Library and the vat sites tomorrow, remember?"

"Of course," Amanda responded. "The fermentation

vats presentation and tour!" Things couldn't be working out more perfectly. This investigation was going to be all wrapped up lickety-split.

"I'll get things ready," Vincent enthused. "I've got some new gadgets I've been working on, and this is just the occasion to test them out. We'll get to the bottom of this in a jiff!"

Amanda hung up, proud of her investigative skills and of her friend Vincent. She knew he would come through with the tech.

She picked up the phone again, started to dial Emily's number, and then hung up. What was the point? She'd fill her in later . . . maybe.

15

Oyster Cove's legendary fermentation vats were a thing of great local pride, second only to the town's fabled curd industry. The Abel Goatslam Memorial Branch Library held in its permanent collection a plethora of historical documents related to the vaulted vats, and today the seventh grade was headed there to hear a lecture all about them. Since the library had been built on the same property that housed those legendary pickle crocks, the seventh-grade class would visit the vats themselves once the lecture was over!

Penelope Offalblog was familiar to everyone who lived in Oyster Cove. She had overcome incredible odds to launch the town's fermentation industry. After townsfolk had laughed at her idea to pickle their way to fame and fortune, Penelope had crafted the great crockery vats with her own hands. At first, she won only regional

Penelope Offalblog
The Pickle Princess

acclaim with her small-batch jars of pickled okra. But as word spread, Penelope's fermented treats—as well as the town's reputation—grew into a national phenomenon. By the end of her career, Penelope had amassed a whopping fourteen-vat empire!

Although the vats had long since fermented their last cucumber and shred of cabbage in the secret brine recipe the Offalblogs had safeguarded for over a century (it remained locked in a safe-deposit box in an undisclosed location), the massive pottery tubs were still a great source of Oyster Cove pride.

Amanda had wonderful memories of touring the vats with her parents as a tot. Today, however, she had far more pressing (and interesting) things to spend her time on than listening to the oft-repeated tale.

As luck would have it, Poppy had signed up to be a chaperone, and after Amanda filled him in on what was what, he'd eagerly agreed to cover for her so she could slip into the library's stacks to investigate Synisteria.

"I've got so much great stuff in here!" Vincent sidled up next to Amanda and motioned to his backpack. "Wait until you see! I tested my new tracking device on my cousin Henthorpe last night. It totally works!" He looked as excited as Amanda felt.

"Let's hope it helps us get to the bottom of this mystery," Amanda whispered back as the two boarded the bus. "Then we can get back to saving Rickie!"

The smell of diesel fuel and pleather seat covers blasted Amanda's senses. But that nasty stench was nothing compared to the fact that the only seats available were directly behind Geri.

Amanda shuffled sideways along the narrow path and plopped down. Vincent followed suit. Nobody made eye contact.

"Is that macramé?" Amanda heard Geri stage whisper. "It looks so very . . . plant-holder-ish. Is it supposed to be a sweater?"

Amanda peered over Geri's shoulder. Of course the subject of Geri's remarks was Cathy Swan. Cathy had the unfortunate bench seat directly in front of OCMS's new

Queen of Mean, and Geri was leaning over the timid girl and muttering awful things.

Amanda strained to hear Geri's furiously whispered assault. She couldn't make out most of it, but managed to pick up the words *upholstery*, *fun with yarn*, *dump truck*, and *polyester parade*.

Cathy reached into her backpack. "Geri, w-would you like a cherry—cream cheese cupcake?" Geri held her nose at the baked morsel as if it were a sandwich bag full of fish emulsion and continued on her rant.

"Ugh!" Amanda balled her fists and summoned up an image of lasagna to keep from going full Bug Girl on the big yellow bus. This public cruelty was absolutely disgusting. How could people sit by and let this happen? She turned to look for her supposed crime-fighting partner. What she saw was Emily ignoring the injustice and focusing on *herself*. As usual. The buoyant blonde was mincing her way down the bus aisle, passing out buttons and smiling her face off to promote her Dancing Queen campaign.

"Seriously?" Amanda sank back into her seat and crossed her arms.

When Emily approached Geri's seat, Amanda looked up. A tiny flicker of hope sparked inside her, a desperate wish that her partner would do the right thing. At last. Instead, Emily paid Geri a compliment. "That necklace is gorgeous," she said.

"Why, thank you," Geri responded. "It was my grandmother's, and it is beautiful if I do say so myself. I wear it with everything."

"Okay," Emily replied disinterestedly. She handed Geri a button. "My buttons aren't as cute as yours," she burbled, making fake sad eyes, "but I tried."

Amanda could not keep quiet any longer. "You *tried*?" she asked, sitting up and looking straight at Emily. "Coulda fooled me."

Then Amanda turned to Geri. "Hey," she said loudly, "you want to leave Cathy alone?"

Geri whipped her head around so fast, Amanda wondered how she didn't get whiplash. "As if I need to listen to you," the awful girl seethed, staring into Amanda's eyes. "Don't you have some dung beetles to tend to or something?"

At the front of the bus, Poppy heard the commotion and lurched to his feet. "Can it back there," he yelled, "or I'll settle your hash and write up slips for the principal! You'll be pounding erasers for a week!" There was a moment of silence. Then Poppy plopped back into his seat and started fidgeting with the antennae on an old transistor radio he'd brought along for no apparent reason at all. His threat seemed to have done the trick—Geri turned back around and gazed out the window. She was remarkably quiet.

Amanda craned her neck to check in on Cathy. She could see that the poor picked-on girl had relaxed, at least a little bit. Her shoulders were no longer scrunched up, and she was reading a book. Good.

When the bus pulled up to the library, the students all shuffled out, ready to learn about the town's pickling past. Mr. Chauncey Kelkenglapher, Oyster Cove's fermentation history expert, was on hand to give the presentation, which added to the anticipation.

One by one the students filed into the library's main auditorium. Amanda and Vincent lagged behind and were the last two in line.

"Poppy, Vincent and I are going on our covert mission now," Amanda whispered to her grandfather, who was busy doing a head count at the door. "We'll be back before you know it!"

"If you're lucky, you'll be done in time to hear about the Brine Flood of 1936," Poppy mused. "The hills smelled of kraut for weeks after those vats breached." He looked off into the distance as if reliving a very fond memory.

"Sounds exciting!" Amanda humored him. "We'll try to make it!"

"Just be back in time for the vat tour. Each of us is getting a mini vat replica filled with pickled artichokes! Oh, and, Vincent, don't forget your homework!"

"What did he mean by that?" Amanda asked as they walked off.

"I have not the foggiest idea," Vincent replied. "Let's go find our criminal!"

The doors to the auditorium swung shut behind them as Amanda and Vincent tiptoed to the library's stacks, where they hoped to discover Synisteria, otherwise known as Ginny Lou, doing her day job.

"Where should we look?" Vincent asked. "She could be anywhere!"

"I think we should just start at the front of the room, and work our way through until we spot someone shelving books."

Amanda had never really considered such people before. She loved going to libraries—this one in particular—and had spent many afternoons pulling out books to read about her favorite subjects. How the books got back on the shelves after people looked at them or checked them out had never been a concern previously.

The two friends walked from aisle to aisle, peering down the long, narrow rows. The library was especially quiet today with nary a browser or borrower to be seen, and Amanda started to get discouraged. What if Ginny Lou only worked part-time? What if she was on her lunch break?

But as they neared the end of the rows, Amanda stopped. All the way down at the end of the row, she saw a woman hunkered over a cart of books.

"Vincent, look!" Amanda pointed to the sign featuring

the Dewey decimal classification at the end of the shelf. "Seven-nine-one-point-four: Motion pictures, radio, and television! She's shelving books about movies!"

"Sinister," Vincent said conspiratorially. "You think she's reading up on horror movies? Like, which ones scare the pants off people?"

"Terrifying! So what's your plan?"

"I just need to dump my tracking device into her bag," Vincent said. "I think that's her purse there, on the bottom of her cart. Once this little number is planted, we can track her whereabouts on my tablet. It's all set up to show us just where she is at all times!"

"Okay, I'll go ask her a question. You sneak around and plop that thing into her purse."

Amanda swallowed hard and started her march down the dark row of books toward the villain, who was currently hefting a tome up onto a shelf almost too high for her to reach.

"Pardon me." Amanda coughed.

"Yes? Can I help you?" The woman looked up. Her name tag read GINNY LOU.

Amanda gulped. "I'm looking for a book about creating aspic salads. My grandmother is crazy about vegetable-and-meat molds and any foodstuffs suspended in Jell-O, and I wanted to find some new recipes."

"Why, you're in the wrong row, dear! The cookbooks are all over in the six-hundred-forties, and I know for a fact that we've got some simply fantastic books on aspic. Just wait until you see what you can make with some peas, a can of tuna, and a gelatin packet! Let me show you!"

Amanda's grandma had been gone for years, but it was true that she had loved aspic. Amanda still recalled the countless shiny, jiggling dishes forced upon the family. Meemaw was always trying to outdo herself, suspending bizarre combinations like meatballs, carrots, and cheese blocks in molded fish shapes. Amanda missed her Meemaw, but the LAST thing she wanted to do was encourage the culinary tradition.

ASPIC SALAD ASSORTMENT

But she allowed Ginny Lou, who seemed helpful and quite friendly, to take her several rows over, hoping that Vincent would be successful in depositing his tracking device into her purse.

"Now, if you'll excuse me," Ginny Lou said sweetly after indicating where Amanda should search, "I've got to shelve tons of quilting books. The Harvest Quilting Bee is coming up, you know. I've never seen such demand in the crafting section!"

Amanda was well aware of the upcoming Bee. She had checked out more than one of those books herself with an eye toward participating in the town-wide art project.

Don't get distracted by the subtle art of quilting, she told herself firmly, refocusing on her task. She had a criminal to bust!

Almost as soon as Ginny Lou had left Amanda to review various salad mold guidelines, Vincent appeared around the corner. He was excited and out of breath.

"Did you do it?" Amanda whispered, putting down *Aspic for Social Occasions*.

"Yes! Take a look!" Vincent pulled his tablet out of his

backpack. A giant red dot bleeped on and off on a map, the address of the library showing above it.

"When she leaves here, we'll be able to track her every move! That is, as long as she's got her purse with her."

Amanda was so proud of Vincent, she gave him a hug. With his tech and her powers, they were going to bust Synisteria and get things back to normal! Amanda NEEDED to solve this mystery quickly so she could move on to other tasks. She had a lake to clean and a cryptid to save!

The two friends slid silently back into the auditorium just as Mr. Kelkenglapher wrapped up his discussion on the merits of probiotics in fermented cabbage.

"Oyster Cove is one of the healthiest towns in the nation," the expert noted, "all thanks to the friendly bacteria our forebearers had swirling around in their bellies."

Poppy patted the seat beside him, and Amanda took it.

"Did you get what you needed?" her grandfather whispered.

Amanda nodded. "Yes. Thanks for your help."

Vincent gave Poppy a thumbs-up, and Amanda smiled widely. She hoped he could see it in the dimly lit auditorium. She still felt a little guilty for storming away from training the other day. It wasn't Poppy's fault that Emily was impossible.

"And did you patch things up with the minor Mega-woman?" Poppy asked.

"No," she admitted.

"Well, don't go chasing any baddies on your own," Poppy cautioned.

Amanda had heard that before. "I've got Vincent," she whispered in Poppy's ear.

Poppy clucked his tongue. "A gadget geek is all well and good, but don't be mistaking him for a partner. You need to get over your ballyhoo and get down to business."

The back of Emily's blonde head was visible in the low light three rows ahead of them. Amanda stared at it. Poppy had never steered her wrong before. She supposed she should heed his advice.

Taking out a pencil and a piece of binder paper, she scribbled a note.

Meet me after school. It's important—for REAL! I have news for you. And WE'VE got a case to solve.

There. She folded the paper into the shape of a ladybug and hid it in her hand.

When the lecture was over and all the students' minds were still lingering on the wonders of probiotics, Amanda waited by the door. Students scuttled past, one by one. When it was Emily's turn, Amanda pretended to trip, careening right into her popular partner.

"Watch it!" Emily hissed, making a show of her attitude.

Emily tried to press on, but Amanda grabbed her arm and crammed the origami note firmly into her partner's hand.

Then she crossed her fingers and hoped that Emily would actually read it.

Waiting for the school day to end was torturous. Amanda was so anxious to get on with the busting of Synisteria that she could not sit still. She fidgeted in her desk until the final bell rang and then paced the halls, hoping that Emily would actually show up to meet her as requested.

"I think Synisteria's home," Vincent said. He was sitting on the floor nearby, pointing at his tablet. The screen showed the red dot blinking in a new spot on the grid. "She hasn't moved from this space for over an hour, and it's not the library."

As Amanda leaned over to look at the new location, she felt a tap on her shoulder. She turned to see not Emily but Cathy Swan timidly standing behind her.

"Are you guys going to monitor Rickets Lake this afternoon?" Cathy asked. "I heard there was another sighting today!"

Amanda felt a pang. She longed to get back to Rickie, and she hated letting Cathy down, but there was so much to do. "Cathy, you'd better go on your own and report back to the Entomological Society," she said. "Vincent and I have some hush-hush business we're working on . . . you know, for a project." *I'm not fibbing*, Amanda told herself. *I'm just choosing my words creatively.*

"Are you sure?" Cathy asked. "Sightings are getting more and more infrequent. You don't want to miss one! And I have a fresh pan of pumpkin-espresso-almond-butter brownies already packed. I made them this morning. I mean, they are FRESH." Amanda could tell that Cathy was pushing past her comfort zone—reaching out to try to make a connection. She promised herself she'd make more time to spend with her and her ridiculously good, floury treats in the future. But right now . . .

"I'm sorry; we really can't," Vincent interjected. "We look forward to reviewing your findings. And if you can save me one of those brownies, I would most certainly appreciate it, because let me tell you—I've consumed plenty of baked goods in my life, and yours are by far the best! And so creative!"

"I sure will, Vincent." Cathy looked both flattered and mildly disappointed, but she was dedicated to her Rickie research and wouldn't let the team down. "Oh, Amanda, thank you for standing up for me on the bus today," she added, then turned and ran away.

"Just in time," Vincent sighed, sounding relieved. "Here comes Emily."

Amanda turned. Sure enough, her partner was stomping toward them from the other direction. Amanda braced for impact.

"What is it now?" Emily hissed, apparently peeved that her precious time was being stolen from her. "These meetings in public places are a trend that needs to cease. What if Manila Florence or Credence Chiffon saw us? Everyone would know."

"Calm down, princess," Vincent blurted. Past experience with Emily had left him nearly immune to her belligerent demeanor. "All that stress will make your roots grow in faster."

"How DARE you!" Emily fumed, narrowing her eyes at Vincent. "I'll have you know that this color is natural!"

"Okay, you two. Zip it," Amanda said. Time, it was a-wasting. "Emily, Vincent and I think we know who's been kidnapping your friends! It's an old-school villain named Synisteria. She's located right here in Oyster Cove, and we need to go round her up right now in order to—"

Emily held up a hand.

"I'm sorry," Emily interrupted. "I have an appointment with Henri au Lait—yes, THE Henri au Lait—to have glamour shots taken this afternoon. And if you think I'm missing this opportunity to go on some random mission with you, then you're crazy. The strings I had to pull to get Henri to fit me in? You have no idea. The dance is crucial. I must win. I must wield that remote control. And besides, I thought you were going to handle this on your own."

Amanda stared at Emily. Then she stared at Vincent, who also was staring at Emily. Then she turned back to stare at Emily again.

"Are you joking right now?" Amanda blurted out. "Emily, these are your friends! They're missing! Your fashion shoot for some dance is not what's important here. I can't even believe I'm hearing this! You *know* Megawoman would disapprove."

"Leave my mother out of this!" Emily snapped. "I've got to go. Henri is waiting, and my makeup and hair team are on set. Besides, my friends are at debate camp. This latest scheme of yours to get me to hang out with you and do your work is, well, sad."

"Please!" Amanda said. "I think that debate camp is a sham. And at this point I'd rather hang out with dryer lint. But you go ahead and get your hair done."

Emily stomped back down the hall. "You don't need me, anyway," she huffed.

"Is that a skirt or a dish towel?" Vincent shouted after Emily, not wanting to let her get away unscathed. "And you'd better get a new crimping iron. The one you're using is giving you split ends!"

Amanda allowed herself to laugh a little. She loved watching Vincent get Emily's goat.

Vincent sat up straighter and cocked his head. "Does she sound sad to you?" he asked.

Amanda frowned and crossed her arms over her chest. Emily never sounded sad. "No," she answered. "She sounds downright deplorable." She turned to Vincent. "It looks like it's up to you and me. But first I have to change."

The custodial closet where Amanda had revealed her true nature to Emily was nearby. She ducked inside and stripped off her outerwear. The close-fitting super-outfit Poppy had designed for her was waiting underneath. It was adorable but offered no protection. This mission was potentially dangerous, and Amanda needed all of her powers at her disposal. She thought hard about her classmates and what she was sure they were suffering at the hands of this film-obsessed fiend. As she focused, she could feel her bug powers taking over. Her exoskeleton hardened into segments along her body. Her antennae protruded from her forehead. Her wings unfurled. Her senses intensified. She stepped out of the closet transformed.

Standing at the corner of Blemish Boulevard and Clotted Court, Bug Girl was in full force and prepared to take

Synisteria out! Vincent stood by her side, anxious to follow her lead in the fight against evil. Together Bug Girl and Vincent looked powerful, strong, and confident.

And before them lay the key to saving their classmates. The duo looked down at Vincent's tablet. His tracking app had led them to the Carbuncle Heights neighborhood on the outskirts of town. It was modest and safe but mostly treeless and bland. The houses had all been built from a cookie-cutter blueprint in the 1950s, and very little had changed since then.

"Look." Vincent pointed. "That's it, there." They'd narrowed the location to the crossroads, and now Vincent had zeroed in on the exact spot.

"It looks so boring," Amanda said, gazing at the peach-colored stucco home. She had expected something a bit more, you know, sinister—dead trees, a moat, perhaps some rotting shutters hanging from one hinge at the sides of blackened, cracked windows. "But we shouldn't let looks deceive us. She's probably in there right this minute, forcing Mikki Folders to watch *The Return of the Foggy Bog Witch* . . . or worse!"

The two started up the walkway and stopped dead in their tracks when they spotted Ginny Lou in her side yard, planting petunias. The villain was hunkered down on her hands and knees, digging in her garden without another care in the world.

"How can she be gardening when our schoolmates are having their eyes assaulted by terrible movies?" Bug Girl hissed.

"Well, it is a pretty amazing garden. It must take quite a bit of tending," Vincent said. "I mean—Sorry. Let's go save the girls!" he added.

Bug Girl was about to respond when she noticed something behind Synisteria. The shed on the side of her house was glowing an eerie green and seemed to be flickering—like a movie was playing inside!

"That does it," Bug Girl said. She launched herself into the air and came in for a smooth yet forceful landing right in front of Synisteria.

"You release those tender young things you've got trapped in that prison," Bug Girl ordered, pointing at the shed.

The startled woman dropped her trowel and stared at the winged tween like she was looking at a ghost. "But . . . but I haven't hardened them off yet!" she replied, not really sure what was happening.

"Okay, I don't even know what you're talking about right now," Bug Girl answered, "but it sounds mean. I'm going to put a stop to this!" She dashed to the glowing shed and easily kicked the door in. What she saw made her suck in her breath. It was unbelievable.

Rows and rows of tiny baby plants lined the shed tables. They glowed in the sunlight filtering in through the semiopaque walls. Green incandescent lights in the corners beamed down onto the seedlings' fragile leaves. In the center of the shed, a small pond rippled as koi and other fish swam back and forth, creating the flickering effect that Bug Girl had been so sure was the glow of a malevolent motion picture tainting children's brains.

"But . . . where are the girls?" Bug Girl asked, turning to face Synisteria and Vincent, who had followed her to the doorway. "Say, do you have a basement? What's going on here?"

The woman shook her head sadly. "There are no girls here, and I don't have a basement. But I think I know who you are, and I'm sure I know why you came," she said. "My reputation lingers, no matter what I do to get past it."

"You mean, you're no longer Synisteria, like, for real?" Vincent asked, putting his tablet in his bag.

"Heavens no," Ginny Lou said. "I'm reformed. I wouldn't hurt a fly! Gardening's my hobby now. Come, come! I'll show you!"

Bug Girl hesitated. But then she remembered that she was Bug Girl. With powers! She could handle herself, and she felt terrible for placing blame where it wasn't warranted. She decided to give Ginny Lou a chance.

She and Vincent stepped into the shed and took a tour of Ginny Lou Johnson's plants. She was growing all sorts of wonderful things—herbs, flowers, water lilies, even a section of succulents.

"I've been branching out," Ginny Lou said with pride as she gave the hero and her friend a tour. "I'm even working with aquaponics now!" She waved her hand toward a tank running along the far wall, filled with beautiful fish.

4. The nutrient-rich water runs through the plants' roots, where it gathers oxygen. The plants extract the nutrients and clean the water.

3. Nutrient-rich water is pumped up to water and fertilize the plants.

5. Clean, oxygen-rich water flows down to the fish tank.

2. Microbes in the water convert the waste into nutrients.

1. The fish produce waste.

Above it was a vegetable garden overflowing with healthy eggplant, tomato, and pepper plants.

"The fish and the plants work together to keep the water clean and pure. It's an amazing filtration system," Ginny Lou told Bug Girl, who was staring, transfixed by the simple yet genius setup.

As fascinating as all of this was, Bug Girl needed to change the subject. She filled Ginny Lou in on the happenings around Oyster Cove regarding the missing students and apologized for her misplaced suspicions.

"Ms. Johnson," Bug Girl finally said after telling her

the whole story, "I'm so sorry for accusing you of kidnapping. I was at an impasse and all signs seemed to indicate that you had gone back to your old habits. . . . I had to investigate."

"No need to apologize, Bug Girl. My deeds were terrible, but I am trying to make up for it. Some of these plants will be donated to gardens around the city to help with beautification projects. And I am quite proud of my work in the library."

"As a reformed villain," Vincent interjected, "do you have any pointers for us? You know, like insights into how villains' brains work, or a list of what we should look out for or beware of?"

"Why yes," Ginny Lou said after a long pause. "Here's a tip: Don't trust anyone. Be very cautious. And be especially suspicious of people who offer you advice before you ask for it. Those characters are covering something up—you mark my words."

Bug Girl and Vincent bid farewell to Ginny Lou Johnson, but not before she let each of them pick a plant from her greenhouse. Vincent chose a ponytail palm while

Amanda opted for a beautifully manicured juniper bonsai tree. They thanked her profusely, then made their way down the walk.

"Aquaponics," Bug Girl said to Vincent, formulating an idea. "We must do some research."

But even though they had a new scientific process to research, when it came to the current crime situation in Oyster Cove, they were back to square one.

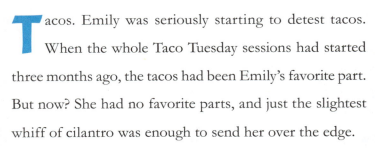

Tacos. Emily was seriously starting to detest tacos. When the whole Taco Tuesday sessions had started three months ago, the tacos had been Emily's favorite part. But now? She had no favorite parts, and just the slightest whiff of cilantro was enough to send her over the edge.

To her, *pico de gallo* tasted exactly like humiliation.

Fear of losing the Dancing Queen title to Geri was making it harder to swallow the reality of losing to Amanda at being super. *Amanda.* The same girl that Emily used to have to keep from eating glue in preschool, the girl Emily always thought of as more timid, awkward, and dorkier than she, now outperformed her in every way as Bug Girl! And although Emily had been trying to feign indifference to save face, it was becoming harder and harder to pretend that she didn't care.

Amanda, however—though she'd been peevish—was

back to playing the perfect hero and supportive partner. Emily wondered what had happened to make her pleasant again.

Each time Emily botched a kick, pulled a power punch, or missed a target, Amanda would yell things like, "Don't worry, you'll get the hang of it!" and "Thirtieth time's a charm!" or "Good try!"

As if.

Amanda wasn't the good sport Poppy and Frida thought she was. Emily was sure that her partner was rubbing her face in it.

Limping over to the taco bar after a bad tumble off the climbing tower, Emily took a seat. She crunched down hard on a tortilla chip and forced herself to watch Amanda blow through the obstacle course their trainers had set up around the Battfields' pool. Amanda's armored feet never touched the ground as she flattened an evil villain pop-up with a single blast from her sound-emitting tymbals, sliced through a barricade with well-aimed acid spittle, flew up the scaffolding tower to retrieve the clue (no climbing, no falling), and located the quarry their trainers had hidden without even bothering to look for the rest of the clues.

"Got it!" Bug Girl yelled, pumping her fist and fluttering a little higher into the sky.

See? Emily breathed out a puff of air. Bug Girl had it all. She didn't need her. Not one little bit.

"Good for you," Emily mumbled sarcastically as she accidentally-on-purpose tipped over the tomatillo salsa that she knew was Amanda's favorite. She brushed a stray hair from her face but apparently had some lingering jalapeño juice on her fingers, because her eyes began to well up.

Bug Girl fluttered down to sit across from her and grabbed a plate. "Are you . . . ?" She leaned closer, squinting, and started to ask Emily something, but they were both interrupted by a rude sound coming from behind them.

"*Pppbbbtbtt!*"

It was Poppy trying to imitate a drumroll. He and Frida had emerged from the house and were standing on either side of the double doors that led to the pool area. Poppy was having trouble making the proper noise because he was grinning so hard. Mostly he was spitting all over himself. Finally he gave up, wiped his mouth, and cleared his throat.

"My girls, we have something very important to announce," he began.

Emily dabbed at her still stinging eyes and gave them a roll. Given Poppy's tendency to ramble, this was probably going to take a while. She allowed herself to fantasize that Poppy was about to announce that nothing in the last few months was real, their moms were not super, she and Amanda had no budding powers, The Exterminator was an actor, and the future they were training for did not exist. She hoped he would say it was all staged—an act for *Reality's on You*, the prime-time practical-joke show where people's worst nightmares were played out for the entertainment of others. Yes. Yes. Soon everything would be back to normal, with her leading the pack and Amanda trailing behind, like a slug. Like it used to be. Like it was supposed to be. But . . .

No.

"We know we've been leaving you girls on your own a lot lately," Poppy prattled. "But it's because we've been doing some other training on the *side*. . . ." He emphasized the word *side*, then bent over double and began slapping his own knees and making barking noises. Emily rolled her eyes again. Finally Poppy righted himself and swabbed away his tears. "That is to say, we've started sidekick training." He beamed. "And we think you're going to get a *kick* out of our first trainee!" Poppy guffawed some more. Frida bit back a rare smile, and the two of them opened wide the French doors leading into the house.

"Presenting . . . Fanboy!" Frida announced with a flourish. She and Poppy clapped loudly. Who should emerge dressed in an upgraded-yet-still-lame green lamé outfit, with his hands in the air, giving a twirl so everyone had to see the full three-hundred-sixty-degree horror of it all? Vincent Verbiglia.

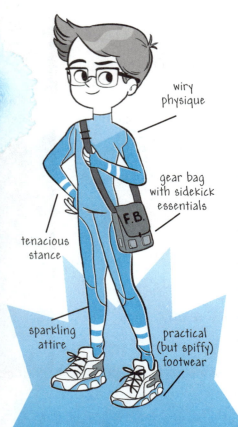

wiry physique

gear bag with sidekick essentials

F.B.

tenacious stance

sparkling attire

practical (but spiffy) footwear

"What? You're official?" Bug Girl squealed. She rushed over to the boy and grabbed his hands. The two of them started jumping up and down in circles, screeching. "But, how?" Amanda asked. "When?"

"This oldster's still got a few tricks up his sleeve," Poppy said. "Frida and I didn't want to announce anything till Vinnie was ready. We've been training him in secret on your days off."

Emily's eyes stung, and this time she knew it was not because of jalapeño juice. She kicked at the ground. "It's not fair!" she screamed. "Amanda gets every-thing!!"

Poppy and Frida, who had been standing with their arms over each other's shoulders looking at the mon-strosity they'd made with obvious pride, turned to gaze at Emily like she was crazy. But Emily knew she wasn't crazy. Amanda had wings. She had real powers. She had a cute custom outfit. She had a good name. And now she had her own *sidekick*?

Emily's chest heaved up and down as she gasped for air. Her eyes glowed. She did not want to be some second-best super! She did not want to compete against some squeaky green sidekick!

Well, Emily thought, fuming, *there is one thing Amanda will never be—she will not be Dancing Queen, and neither will Geri.*

She stomped and kicked again. This time she hit a small piece of lava rock that had strayed onto the patio and sent it sailing. The light, porous stone was launched with such velocity that it sliced through the walls of the pool house before traveling another thousand feet and lodging in a large crustacean statue.

Her vision blurred. She saw Bug Girl lift off of the ground and hover closer to their trainers, looking alarmed.

Then she saw nothing but red.

Emily's tantrum measured five-point-seven on the Richter scale and made the evening news. Nobody could figure out how an earthquake could be centered beside the Battfields' pool house. There was no fault line there.

But Amanda knew what was at fault. And she was trying hard not to think about it. After flying Poppy, Frida, and Vincent to safety, she'd returned to check on Emily and survey the damage. She was a little worried that Emily might hurt herself. But mostly she was annoyed that the selfish brat was having a hissy fit just because Vincent basically got a new and improved outfit. *I mean, get over it already!*

As soon as she made sure Emily was okay—the pretty blonde was just standing there, smoldering in the rubble she'd created—Amanda had flown home. There was no talking to that girl. And no way was she going to help

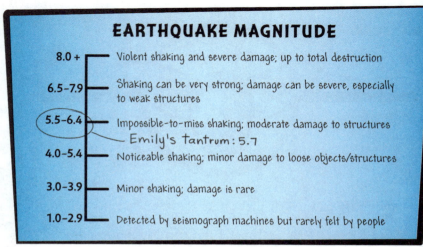

EARTHQUAKE MAGNITUDE

8.0+ — Violent shaking and severe damage; up to total destruction

6.5–7.9 — Shaking can be very strong; damage can be severe, especially to weak structures

5.5–6.4 — Impossible-to-miss shaking; moderate damage to structures
— Emily's tantrum: 5.7

4.0–5.4 — Noticeable shaking; minor damage to loose objects/structures

3.0–3.9 — Minor shaking; damage is rare

1.0–2.9 — Detected by seismograph machines but rarely felt by people

clean up the mess she'd made. But in that moment before she left, as she watched smoke pour out of Emily's ears, Amanda had made a conscious decision to focus on something else. She was sick of trying to make Emily be better. Luckily there was plenty of other stuff to occupy her mind—so much so that she spent the entire night in front of her mother's computer, doing research.

When the sun came up, Amanda didn't know it. It was only when Poppy came down into her mother's lair with a bowl of Cream of Wheat and a mug of tea that she realized she'd been awake all night.

"You look terrible," Vincent said when she arrived at school. He never minced words. "Not as bad as the Battfields' patio but, you know, bad."

"I know," Amanda yawned. "No sleep. Here. Look at this." She handed over the schematics she'd drawn up in the wee hours of the morning. Vincent unrolled them. His eyes flicked quickly back and forth over the diagram. They opened wider as he took in the info, and a smile spread across his face. "Is this . . . ?"

"It's a plan to clean up Rickets Lake . . . and save Rickie." Amanda smiled back and wiped her puffy eyes. "You like it?"

"I. Love. It." Vincent was trembling with excitement. "Aquaponics? Bioremediation? You are a science miracle, Amanda Price! And this plan? It's pure genius. But where will you—"

The bell rang before Vincent could ask his question.

Amanda took back the plan and rolled it up as she hurried to class. Vincent trotted along beside her.

"Oh, before I forget, I logged on to the attendance records this morning and saw that two more girls were absent yesterday," Vincent whispered. "Margaret Mullens and Frances Bantagram."

The news hit Amanda hard. While she was drawing up

plans to save the lake (and trying to forget about Emily) she had shoved aside the fact that they were still nowhere on solving the mystery of the missing girls. Suddenly her eyelids felt like sandbags. Her head pounded. Her sensilla tingled. . . .

What?

Behind her, she heard an unwelcome sound.

"Step aside, please." Geri shoved past them and Amanda felt another prickling in her antennae. She blinked rapidly, then stopped and leaned against the wall to press her palms into her eye sockets. *I'm just exhausted*, she told herself. And so over Geri.

Vincent stood in front of her, his forehead wrinkled with worry. "Are you okay? Is this about her?" He angled his head in Geri's direction. "You can't let her get to you like this!"

"I know." Amanda blinked again. "It's not that. I'm just tired is all." She closed her eyes and thought about springy ramen noodles to try to stop the tingling. The feeling was beginning to fade when a repugnant stench made her nostrils curl. It smelled like burnt hair and curry.

She thought it might be a super-side effect, but she heard Vincent gasp a little . . . and then gag.

Amanda forced her eyes open, and what she saw made her draw in a huge breath, which was a mistake. Hoagie Joe, the cafeteria cook, was standing right in front of them, and the scent of cafeteria slop coming off him was so thick, Amanda felt like it was coating her tongue. Her eyes watered. She looked for a way out, but the large man stepped closer, pinning her and Vincent to the wall. Amanda held her breath.

"You should follow her," Hoagie Joe whispered to the two conspiratorially. His voice sounded like rocks breaking.

Vincent let out a squeak. Amanda could see that his eyes were locked on a mustard stain on Hoagie Joe's collar. She knew he didn't dare breathe for fear of having an asthmatic attack. He was turning purple.

"Who?" Amanda choked out. She put her hand over her nose and mouth.

"Geraldine," Hoagie Joe grumbled. "After school. Watch where she's going."

"You mean Geri?" Amanda risked a breath. She

looked down the hall in the direction Geri had just gone. She was nowhere to be seen. "Why should we follow her?" Amanda preferred to avoid that unpleasantness when possible. Why would she want to poke a hornet's nest?

"Those girls that are missing. They started disappearing when she showed up," Hoagie Joe rasped.

Amanda risked another breath. "That's right. They did. But how do *you* know girls are missing?" *And why are you trying to help us?* she wondered.

"Lunch tickets," Hoagie Joe rumbled. "My lunch-ticket count is off. Been off since she arrived." He scratched his elbow, and a dried bit of gravy peeled off and hit the floor with an audible thunk.

"Okay!" Amanda agreed. "We'll do it." She saluted the man in his not-so-white chef whites, hoping that he would feel dismissed and leave. Miraculously, he did. The big oaf gave a nod, loosening a bit of brisket from his hairnet, and shambled away.

"Puh!" Vincent let his breath out and slid to the floor, gasping for air. "You're not actually going to follow Geri, are you?" he panted.

Amanda wasn't sure. She reached up to feel the spots where her antennae emerged. Those tingles she'd been feeling happened whenever Geri was around. Maybe Hoagie Joe was on to something. Maybe Geri was more than just mean.

"Vincent, my gut tells me that we are on the road to success and rescue!" she chirped. Her newly appointed sidekick could not respond. He was too busy sucking on his inhaler.

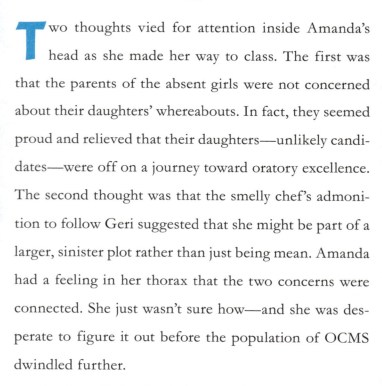

Two thoughts vied for attention inside Amanda's head as she made her way to class. The first was that the parents of the absent girls were not concerned about their daughters' whereabouts. In fact, they seemed proud and relieved that their daughters—unlikely candidates—were off on a journey toward oratory excellence. The second thought was that the smelly chef's admonition to follow Geri suggested that she might be part of a larger, sinister plot rather than just being mean. Amanda had a feeling in her thorax that the two concerns were connected. She just wasn't sure how—and she was desperate to figure it out before the population of OCMS dwindled further.

So when Cindy Cindindermann failed to show up for math class, Amanda couldn't take any more. Her hand shot into the air and she requested a bathroom pass from

Mr. Eggschaff. Then she headed straight for the office, determined to look for some proof. If there was no official record of Obfuscation and Verbosity Debate Camp, then she would know her instinct was correct.

Amanda slipped into the office as quietly and invisibly as possible. She had to act fast—bathroom passes only allowed her so much time! She surveyed her surroundings, and boy, was she in luck—the office was empty and a stack of files was piled on the attendance clerk's desk in an over-flowing bin marked ABSENCES. Amanda's heart raced. She was taking a risk by reading confidential files. What if she got caught? What would her excuse be? Amanda pushed her fears out of her mind. The information inside those manila envelopes would get her one step closer to solving this mystery.

First file up: Sadie Bimmins. *To Whom It May Concern,* the handwritten note on the top began. *Please take this as notice that our Sadie will be absent from school for at least two weeks as we take a tour of the rain forests of Peru. She should get extra credit for this trip, by the way, because it's science. Sincerely, Bruno Bimmins.*

"Please," Amanda snorted. "Sadie wouldn't set foot in a park, much less a rain forest." She slapped the folder down. Next up was Koky Masterbland.

To Whom It May Concern, the note began. *Koky won't be in school for an indefinite period, as she is in New York studying 1960s pop art's lasting effects on American advertising culture.*

"What? She's thirteen! That sounds a bit advanced to me," Amanda spurted. This whole thing was fishy.

One by one, she reviewed the absent girls' folders. Each excuse was more far-fetched than the last. Most important, each note was handwritten in loopy script and each *i* was dotted with a tiny circle. Amanda bet that a handwriting expert could prove beyond a shadow of a doubt that they had all been penned by the same person! The notes proved that there was no camp—and that a single person was behind the disappearances.

Amanda had known those students weren't debate-camp caliber. . . . Imagine Frances Bantagram trying to argue for anything other than the banning of jelly shoes? But those excuses! What was up with the principal buying these tall tales?

"I mean, Vivienne Fud is suddenly a foreign exchange student in Taiwan? They would send her back in a day," Amanda said to herself as she slid the folders back into the bin.

Closing her eyes so she could listen to her inner voice a little more closely, Amanda thought long and hard about her encounter with Hoagie Joe. She got mixed signals from the slimy cook, like a positive and negative chemical reaction at the same time—something she had never encountered before. Creepy (and smelly) as he was, deep down Amanda had a feeling that his advice about Geri was right on the money.

Amanda's sensors had been going off wildly all year and almost always in the vicinity of the uppity transfer student. It all added up to Geri being no good. She had to be connected to the disappearances, just as Hoagie Joe suggested.

"She probably dots her *i*'s with circles," Amanda mumbled.

And Emily was her new BFF. . . .

Amanda shook her head. Emily's new pal was more

than just mean. She was downright dastardly! But she didn't have real proof . . . not yet.

Silently, Amanda slipped out of the office. She needed to talk to Emily ASAP. She was going to corner her contrary partner as soon as she spotted her, no matter where it happened. Even if it was in front of the entire student council, the dance committee, and, yes, the eighth graders! She had to make sure Emily was there when the pieces of the puzzle fell together and they caught Geri in the act.

She wanted to see the look on her ex-bestie's face.

The bell rang just as Amanda got back to class. She fought her way through the throng of exiting kids to hand the bathroom pass back to Mr. Eggschaff. The teacher grumbled something about how long students took in the loo, but Amanda wasn't listening. She was scanning the crowd for Emily.

All around her, students poured into the halls. Everyone was buzzing. Rumors about the missing girls had been circling since last week. Today they were flying faster than spit wads in science class! And each person had a different idea about where the girls had gone.

"It was an alien invasion," Enstrelle Pwistrax hissed to her group of friends.

"No, I heard they're all part of a government program to start a colony on the moon," Conchita Mendez replied.

Amanda stifled a laugh and kept scanning the crowd for Emily.

"Actually," Lawrence Confetti-Bendelson said, "their fate is clear. The monster of Rickets Lake is responsible for the disappearances. And if we don't do something soon to stop the beast, more of our friends will end up as lunch!"

The students surrounding Lawrence gasped.

Amanda gasped, too, but for a different reason. She knew Rickie wasn't the cause of this. She knew it deep down in her heart. Rickie was misunderstood and beautiful. He was a victim himself and already endangered. But with a rumor like this gaining traction, Rickie's situation could become even graver.

Once more, Amanda felt herself pulled in two directions. She took her rolled-up plans from her backpack and clutched them close to her chest but kept scanning the crowded halls for Emily.

"What's shakin'?"

Amanda was so lost in thought that even Vincent's friendly voice made her jump.

"Oh, I just . . . I just don't even know what to do first," Amanda said. "I need to talk to Emily."

Vincent wrinkled his nose.

"And I've got to get going on that lake cleanup."

"You're darn right about that." Sh'Shelle appeared out of nowhere. Her brown eyes were wide with worry. "I've been looking for you guys everywhere. Rickie sightings are way down, and the toxin levels in my latest water samples are off the charts. I think Rickie's in trouble." She held out vials of the poisoned water.

Vincent and Amanda exchanged a look. Amanda's decision was made.

Under the veil of darkness, Bug Girl took flight. Her wings buzzed over a sleepy Oyster Cove toward the hill where Penelope Offalblog's legendary crockery vats sat nestled behind the Abel Goatslam Memorial Branch Library.

Bug Girl had proven in her training sessions with

Poppy and Frida that she had a lot of strength. She could lift any weight they asked her to; she'd held hundreds of pounds over her head. Once, her trainers took her to the wrecking yard and pointed at two junked cars. They asked her to pick them up and throw them at a target seventy-five yards away, and she had done it with no problem! But fermentation vats were a whole new thing.

"Ants," she said to bolster herself as she circled in for a landing by the vats. Everyone knew that ants regularly lifted one thousand times their own weight. It was how they transported food and supplies to their colonies. Sure it was astounding, but for them, and for Bug Girl, it was perfectly normal.

"I have the strength of an ant and I'm going to use it," Bug Girl said to herself. She needed the reassurance. Because, although she had proven her strength during training sessions, she had never tested it while flying. This would be something new.

Bug Girl took a deep breath to calm her nerves and pulled a prepared note out of her costume pocket. She taped the message to the Penelope Offalblog Fermentation Vats Statue.

I borrowed 3 crockery Vats 4 a good cause! I'll bring them back, I promise. —BG

She wrapped a cable she'd brought around one of the giant containers, secured it, and fastened it beneath her wings like a harness. Then she beat her wings with all her might. After a few bumpy liftoffs that ended in the vat thudding back down to the ground, she grunted, "I can do this!" and pushed even harder. Knowing what was at stake, she willed her wings to flap faster and harder than they ever had before, and slowly she gained altitude.

Once she had mustered a little momentum, Bug Girl soared through the air toward Rickets Lake with the vat hanging beneath her. When she arrived at the murky, littered shore, she lowered the vat gingerly into the water, making sure it wasn't completely submerged and that she was able to access its drainage port and connector valves.

She repeated the process with the second vat, then a third, and finally got to work hooking up the giant containers.

She felt slightly guilty that she had tampered with a local landmark but reminded herself that once her project was complete, she could just fly the vats back to their original location and there would be no harm done. "I haven't done any permanent damage," she said out loud.

Sh'Shelle's lab analysis of the Rickets water samples had shown that the polluted water could be cleaned using microorganisms. They would basically "eat" the pollutants—breaking down nitrogen and creating oxygen. After that, filtration and sunlight would remove the rest of the toxins. Amanda had diagrammed what she'd named the *Bioremediation System Phase One* ("BSP1" for short)—a pool filter with a solar battery that would pump water slowly into one vat, where beneficial bacteria was growing. (She had taken samples from healthy Snifferveldt Swamp on the other side of town.) The water would pass through a tube and into the second vat as it was cleaned and then into the third "holding vat," where sunlight would finish the job. Then the clean water would flow back into the lake and the process would repeat until all the water was clean. Controlling the bacteria in the vats would be important. She had to make sure they kept the right balance so they could restore, rather than deplete, the oxygen. She wanted to be sure that Rickie (and any other animals that might live in the lake's fetid depths) could breathe!

Bug Girl spent the night putting her plan into action, and when everything was ready, she dumped the Snifferveldt samples into the first tank. When the sun came up, the solar battery on the pool pump would kick in and, she hoped, the filtration process would begin.

"Dear Rickie, I wish for you clean water and a home you can be proud of," she said toward the center of the dismal, stinking lake. She sprinkled a handful of Cricket Crispies into the water for good luck. Some hopeful bubbles rose to the surface and popped. Had Rickie heard her? Was he down there watching?

Fluttering up, she took one last glance inside the first vat. "Get growing, you megamicrobes! Small is mighty! And you have some big work to do."

She hovered close to the ground to put up one last note, taping it securely to the first vat. This one read: BSP1 EXPERIMENT IN PROGRESS. DO NOT TOUCH! And with that, she buzzed home for some much-needed sleep. Tomorrow was another day, and she knew it would involve more sinister goings-on than it would friendly bacteria.

BIOREMEDIATION SYSTEM
• Phase One •

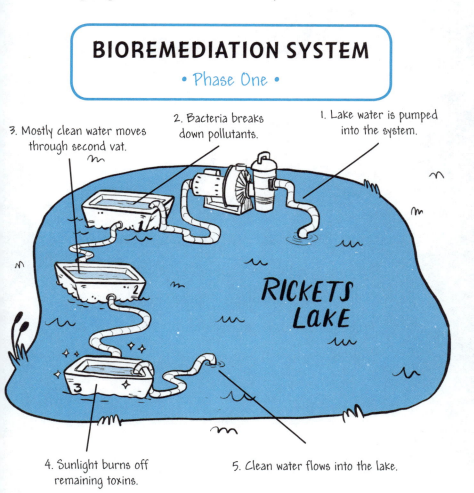

3. Mostly clean water moves through second vat.

2. Bacteria breaks down pollutants.

1. Lake water is pumped into the system.

RICKETS LaKE

4. Sunlight burns off remaining toxins.

5. Clean water flows into the lake.

ANT

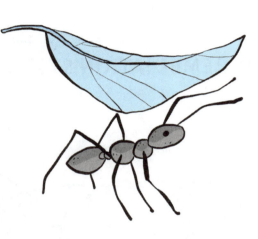

Fun Bug Fact: An ant can lift 1,000 times its own weight over its head—the equivalent of a 100-pound girl lifting 100,000 pounds, or 50 tons. (That's about the weight of a Boeing 747 or fifty blue whales!)

20

"**I**f elected at the dance tonight, I promise to bring an end to mismatched prints throughout the halls of Oyster Cove Middle School," Geri read from the pink index cards in her hand. She was standing at a podium in the school cafeteria, presenting her case to the student body, telling them all exactly why she should be crowned Disco Daze Dancing Queen.

Leaning up against the milk dispensary, Emily had her hands balled so tightly into fists that they had turned an eerie white. She was livid. It took every ounce of restraint she could muster to keep from kicking the dairy case into a useless ball of metal. She was scheduled to make her own speech immediately following Geri's, and she needed to calm down if she was going to be a convincing candidate.

"I'll make sure we have mandatory fashion training

sessions with an emphasis on proper accessorizing," Geri continued. "And I'll implement a 'two strikes, you're out' policy on fashion tickets." This speech was getting worse by the second. Emily gazed around the lunchroom. Every student was openmouthed, not really sure that what they were witnessing was real. Verona LaTrine was frozen in such terror that a forkful of macaroni hovered between her tray and her mouth, quivering like a jellyfish. A group of black-clad redheads glowered in the corner. It was a bad scene.

"And finally," Geri said cheerily, "I promise that, if you vote for me, as Dancing Queen I will put an end to all of these tacky earthquakes."

Emily froze. Did Geri actually look directly at her when she said that? How could she know? Maybe she was just making eye contact with her audience, like any good public speaker is supposed to do, but it sure felt . . . loaded.

"You may applaud now," Geri said. The cafeteria sat silent for a few brief, horrible seconds and then erupted into insane cheers and claps. Emily didn't get it. Two seconds ago everyone looked like they were trapped in a crypt with a dead body, and now they were acting like this was the best moment of their lives! Did Geri really have that much control? Was this fear at work?

Turning to her right, Emily saw a poster for Geri's Dancing Queen campaign. In the glamour shot, she was holding the collar of her shirt in her fingers and had a sequined top hat tilted just so on top of her perfectly coiffed head. Emily fumed with such intensity that the edges of the poster began to curl up from the heat before bursting into flames.

"Rats," Emily muttered as the fire alarm screeched to life. Groaning students pushed their chairs away from their tables and shuffled outside to await further instructions.

Now Emily wouldn't even be able to give her speech.

Her day—no, her life—was ruined. With

HATS OFF TO THE DANCING QUEEN

her speech unheard, the vote at tonight's dance would be tallied based solely on the display of bullying she had just witnessed.

Surely the students of Oyster Cove remembered what a bright light Emily had always been in their otherwise boring lives. Surely they would choose her just because she was Emily Battfield, student royalty. She had to win. She HAD to.

She was visualizing her victory and imagining exactly what it would feel like to push the button on the disco ball remote when she felt a tap on her shoulder.

"Emily!" A gnat-like buzzing sounded in her ear. "Emily, snap out of it!" The buzz wouldn't go away. In fact, it seemed to be getting louder. And more persistent.

She whirled around and came face-to-face with Amanda.

"Oh, it's you. I'm beginning to think you got that supername because you BUG people so much," Emily seethed, crossing her arms in a huff. "What do you want now?"

"I'm trying to clean up several messes," Amanda whispered. "And I need your help! We're partners, remember?" Amanda paused. "Besides, I have something I can't wait to tell you about your new best friend."

Emily looked away. Amanda could be pretty convincing, but she still felt sure that Bug Girl did not need her help for anything.

"Seriously, Emily, I think I know who's behind the disappearances. You aren't going to want to hear this, but . . . I think it's Geri."

Friend. Geri. Emily closed her eyes for a moment to keep from torching anything else.

Initially she'd had hopes that she and Geri might be friends—real friends. But those hopes were dashed the minute Geri started to compete against her. Amanda would never understand how things worked in popular circles—the pressure she was under. But Emily should have known better. *Friends.* That was a laugh.

"What makes you think that Geri's involved?" Emily asked.

"I got a tip. And my sensilla freak out whenever I'm

around her," Amanda whispered. "We need to follow her after school. We need to see what she's up to."

Emily yawned. "I'm sick of following Geri." Emily had been following her since she arrived. "You should follow her on your own, and take your emerald sidekick with you. It'll be a nice little project for you both. I've got to get ready for the dance tonight." Emily tried to sound like she meant it—but she knew her Dancing Queen dream was already dashed.

"Emily, I know the dance is important to you, but a sidekick is not the same as a partner!" Amanda hissed. "I need *your* help. I can't do this without you."

Emily gulped. Amanda appeared to be completely serious.

"If I'm right about Geri being responsible for the missing girls," Amanda said, "and I'm pretty sure that I am, then you'll not only be a hero for rescuing your friends. You'll also be erasing any and all obstacles between you and the crown at the dance. You'll be *arresting* your competition, so to speak."

Emily gulped again. Maybe Amanda *did* understand what the dance meant to her. "That's right," she mumbled. "I would be the only one in the running to wield that remote! If Geri's guilty, she'll get suspended— or worse! She'll get sent away to some camp where they'll make her wear a burlap jumpsuit and ugly shoes and adopt a better attitude. She'll have to eat food worse than what Hoagie Joe dishes out. She'll be surrounded by people way meaner than she could ever dream of being! And I have to admit: I do miss my entourage. If you've really got evidence that Geri is behind it, then I should do my part."

Emily turned to face Amanda with a genuine smile on her face. Amanda's face was expressionless.

"Yes," Emily said. "I will follow her with you! And I will bring back those girls, and everything will go back to normal." Emily could picture it—with Geri gone and her crew back, she would rule the school once more.

Amanda sighed audibly.

"She'll forfeit," Emily said with a giggle, ignoring the resigned look on Amanda's face. A forfeit wasn't

the most satisfying of victories, but it was a victory. She skipped away down the hall, picturing the brighter days ahead.

"So I'll see you after school?" Amanda called after her. "At the tennis courts?"

Emily didn't bother to answer.

21

500, 537, 624, 756, 924. Amanda watched with satisfaction as the numbers on the tiny biocounter she had clipped to her sweatshirt clicked up and up and up. The number of microbes in the repurposed vat were growing exponentially! The colony was thriving, and each one of those new little babies was eating up filth and turning it into something good. Just thinking about it made Amanda's heart sing.

Carefully, so as not to call attention to herself, Amanda tilted the counter so Vincent could read it from his seat across the aisle in Ms. Pomfrey's English class. Vincent smiled back and gave Amanda a thumbs-up under his desk. He'd made the biocounter himself, hooking it up to a sensor in the crocks at Rickets Lake to provide real-time readouts. It was just the kind of thing a great sidekick did.

At least something is going according to plan, Amanda

thought. She'd been watching the microbe numbers grow all day. And it was really helping take her mind off of other things; namely, her upcoming surveillance mission with Emily. *That* had her gnawing her fingernails to nubs.

It was sad, really, the way Amanda had finally convinced Emily to work with her—by making it about the dance. But if that was what it took . . .

Time dragged during last period. When the biocounter tipped over the one trillion mark, there were still thirty seconds to go in the school day.

Finally, the bell rang.

"Look: one trillion!" Amanda pointed out the milestone to Vincent in a whisper as she started toward the tennis courts. Vincent quietly cheered. Then he wished Amanda luck.

"I'd come along, but I don't want to trigger another episode from Emily," Vincent said. "Oh, but I did manage to slip a tracker into Geri's handbag." He smiled coyly. "You're welcome."

Vincent handed Amanda a small tablet with a blinking red dot. It was just like the one they'd used to track

Synisteria. Then, without another word, Vincent ducked behind a large sequined banner encouraging OCMS students to SHUFFLE ON OVER to the Disco Daze Dance and disappeared.

Emily was waiting at the courts with her arms folded across her chest. "Let's get this over with," she said. "I need to practice my acceptance speech and get ready for the dance tonight."

Thanks to Vincent's tracking tools, it took less than fifteen minutes for Emily and Amanda to locate their target.

"What is this place?" Emily said, looking askance at the sign on the building. "Disgruntled Pastures? Is it some sort of dairy farm? I think your toady has totally led us

astray." She handed the tablet back to Amanda and sniffed dismissively.

Amanda squinted up at the building and bit her lip. She looked at the blinking red dot on the screen. She didn't doubt Vincent's tools . . . but the senior living center in front of her didn't look like the kind of place a girl like Geri would hang out.

"Let's just take a look." Amanda led Emily around the side of the building to peek in one of the windows. What they saw was pretty much what you'd expect—the silver-haired, all-female set inside were napping in easy chairs or gathered around tables playing mah-jongg and canasta.

"See?" Emily said, all snotty.

The last thing Amanda wanted to do was admit that Emily was right. Luckily she didn't have to, because at that moment her antennae tingled and Geri appeared, carrying a tray. She made her way from senior to senior and began to place what looked like . . . crowns on their heads.

"Um . . ." Amanda wasn't sure what to say.

"That's weird," Emily finished for her.

"Maybe she volunteers here?" Amanda offered. "Maybe it's a birthday?" But nothing about what she was looking at made sense. Her sensilla were really starting to smart.

Geri continued to move around the room, talking softly to the nine bent-over women, smoothing their hair and placing thin metal bands covered in pretty gems on their heads.

Amanda blinked twice, hoping that what she was seeing would miraculously be explained. Was it possible that Amanda had the new girl pegged wrong? "What is your friend doing? I mean, it looks like she's being . . . nice?"

"That's not like her." Emily planted her hands on her hips. "She's probably just trying to *act* nice to get people to vote for her!"

"But . . ." That didn't add up. "There isn't anyone here from school to see this. And I thought *fear* was her thing." Amanda kept studying the confusing scene. Emily was silent.

When all of the elderly gamers were wearing crowns, Geri took her tray back to the kitchenette. She pushed some buttons on an espresso machine.

Huh? Now she was making them coffee?

"What is going *on*?" Emily demanded.

"Wait a second." Amanda put one hand on Emily's arm to try to keep her calm, then she bent closer to the window. She leaned so close that her breath started to make little spots of fog appear on the glass. "Look!"

Emily saw what Amanda was pointing to immediately.

"Those shoes are not orthopedic!" Emily gasped.

Beneath the tables, the footwear of the canasta players was highly unexpected. Nothing about what was covering the feet of the elderly women was remotely appropriate for bunions or preventing back pain. There were platform shoes and sparkle sneakers and chunky lace-up boots.

"We've got to get in there and get a closer look!" Amanda said. "I don't think Geri's making lattes!" Amanda strode into the sterile-smelling building with Emily right behind her. There was nobody sitting at the front desk, so the girls marched right back to the rec room to see just what in the blazes was going on, busting through the accordion doors together. A few heads turned slowly. But if any of the girls inside were surprised, they didn't show it.

In the kitchenette, Geri was still pushing buttons. *That's no espresso machine*, Amanda thought as the device began to blink and glow.

Then she noticed that the crowns on the players' heads were lighting up in the same rhythm as the machine. And so was the stone in Geri's necklace!

"Hey, those are the shoes that Trixie Symcox wore to Babs Hedgepeth's pool party!" Emily pointed at a pair of wedge sandals worn by a crowned woman with dyed-blue hair. At the same moment, Amanda recognized Lorricent's palm-tree earrings dangling from the withered lobes of a woman with a walker. "That old lady stole Trixie's shoes!" Emily bleated.

"Nope," Amanda said. "That *is* Trixie."

Emily let her mouth fall open and stay that way. She looked at each of the women wearing the illuminated crowns and began talking softly to herself and ticking off the names of the missing girls on her fingers.

Amanda looked from the card players to Geri and back. With each pulse of light, Geri seemed to be glowing more brightly. The mean queen stood straighter. Her cheeks grew rosy. Her eyes sparkled. She started to giggle.

"Holy crudbusters! She's draining the life right out of them!" Amanda exclaimed.

"Ew!" Emily shouted, nostrils flaring. "That is *not* okay."

Geri stopped sniggering and looked up from her youth-capturing device. She blinked her green eyes and focused on Emily and Amanda. She didn't look at all surprised to see the two of them there together. In fact, she let out another tiny giggle and stretched out her arms, like she'd just awakened from the world's most refreshing nap and was delighted to see them.

"Well, look who's here!" Geri cooed. "Come to join the party?" She took a step forward. So did Emily.

"I'm not joining anything *you're* a part of!" Emily sneered. "Tell her, Amanda!"

But Amanda could not tell Geri anything.

Amanda could not think.

Amanda could not move.

Amanda's eyes were locked on a purple velvet couch in the corner. It was calling to her. It was beckoning her close, begging her to lie down. The settee smelled like everything good in the world. . . . It was . . . it was . . . irresistible . . . and Amanda could think of nothing else!

22

"**J**ust exactly what do you think you're doing, anyway?"

Emily looked from Geri to Amanda. She wasn't sure which one of them she was directing her question toward; she just knew she needed some answers. Pronto!

If you asked her, *both* Geri and Amanda were acting completely unacceptably. Geri, who looked fresher than a dewdrop, since she'd apparently just drained the living daylights out of the popular population of OCMS, was smiling coyly at her own reflection in the glass door of a defibrillator cabinet. Amanda, who had demanded they follow Geri into this creepy home in the first place, seemed to think her job was done and was reclining on some purple velvet fortune-teller's couch. *What is she thinking?* Emily wondered. *This is no time for a nap!*

"Amanda!" Emily snapped.

Geri shushed her. She nodded her head toward one

of the sleeping seniors. "Don't get so wound up. Anger causes wrinkles, you know."

Emily shot Geri a look. "Shut. Up. I'm twelve. I don't care about wrinkles."

Geri winced. "When you get to be *my* age, you will." Geri turned back to her reflection in the glass, touching the outside corners of her eyes and running a finger over her eyebrows admiringly.

Emily squinched up her brow. She stared at her archrival. Geri looked like a typical seventh grader.

"What are you talking about?" Emily asked. "How old can you be? Are you fourteen? Did you get held back or something?"

"I'm twelve!" Geri chirped. "Times ten," she added more softly.

Emily did the math. "What? You're *one hundred and twenty*?" Emily looked around the room, hoping she hadn't offended any of the residents. Then she looked at Amanda to see if she was catching this. Geri was some sort of ancient youth-sucker! It didn't seem possible.

But Amanda was in full sprawl on the couch. Her eyes

were closed, and she was mumbling something about the incredible scent. What was her *deal*?

"If I can look like this, what does it matter?" Geri snapped. "Age is just a number!"

Emily was getting seriously annoyed. "Yeah, but you're one hundred and twenty and you hang out with seventh graders. Isn't that sorta . . . pathetic?"

Geri scowled. "Listen, girlie, I only put up with you and your little 'friends' so I can get this glow." She waved her hand in front of her face. "You think I like hobnobbing with you tykes, gossiping about Skip and Tommy and all the other schlubs that go to your dump of a school, pretending to care about your little nitwit problems? I can't wait to get away from those middle-school creeps, and I can't wait to get away from you!"

Geri yelled the last word, then shut her eyes to try to gather herself. She took a deep breath.

"I've been working at this antiaging technique for a long time, experimenting with different youth regeneration systems along the way. Oh, lots of the procedures restored my youth and energy, but in the end something

would always fizzle and fade and I would have to go back to the drawing board. I've been slipping from town to town, tapping into various youthful essences and tinkering with my methods for decades. Over the years, I've gleaned a lot of knowledge. But it was a lot of endless work. Until now." Geri clapped her hands together and revealed a sinister grin. "Now, at long last, I've discovered a way to make my youth *permanent*!"

"Not if I can help it!" Emily spat back. She cringed at the thought of just how many middle schoolers Geri must have turned into raisins while perfecting her technique. She wasn't exactly sure how she *was* going to stop the ancient tween, but she was going to stop her. *Maybe I can hit her with something.* Emily looked around the room for something to throw, while Amanda continued to lounge on the sofa like it was her day off. *Come on!*

"Hey, Amanda, get off that couch!" Emily shouted. "We've got work to do!"

Amanda didn't move.

But the couch did.

While Emily watched, tapping her foot impatiently, the couch twitched and began to close! *It couldn't be. . . .*

"Amanda, get off that dang couch!" Emily yelled.

Amanda wasn't being lazy; she was about to be *eaten* by a *sofa*! Emily lurched toward the piece of purple furniture, ready to pull Amanda out of danger, but Geri stepped in front, blocking her way.

"Not so fast, princess."

"Princess?" Emily snarled. "Excuse me?" She tried to step around Geri, but each time Emily moved, Geri moved, too. And so did the couch! It was closing on Amanda more quickly now. Plus the plush upholstery appeared to be growing green and red tendrils. Emily didn't know a lot about nature, but she did know that the brightly colored stuff was usually poisonous.

"Get out of my way!" Emily snapped, giving Geri a shove. Geri stumbled back, and Emily managed to grab one of Amanda's arms before she was completely swallowed. She pulled, but nothing happened. "What is this, a flytrap?" she shouted.

Geri laughed and dusted herself off. "More like a bug trap . . . a Bug *Girl* trap." She continued to chortle to herself at the sheer genius of her plan. It had everything an evil plan needed: irony, danger, purple velvet. . . .

Emily let go of Amanda's arm and spun around to glare at Geri. "But how did you know she was—"

"Bug Girl? Oh, I know all about Bug Girl," Geri said, winding a lock of her hair around her finger. "After the decades I've spent in the ultravillain business, I've got a knack for picking out heroes incognito. It's pretty easy, really. They have do-gooder attitudes and miss events where everyone else is present, then pop up right after the hero has vanquished the villain or rescued whatever stupid person was in danger and blather, 'Oh, did I miss something?' Please! It's so obvious!

"And I know all about you, too. What's your supername

again? Oh, that's right—you don't have a name. But that silver unitard of yours is so stereotypical that you might consider 'the Blasé Blaze' or 'Princess Predictable,' or how about just 'Yawn'? I can't even begin to tell you how desperately dull that shimmery suit is—almost as bad as your transfixed little partner's ice-skating costume. You both deserve too many fashion tickets for me to even write."

Geri paused.

"But speaking of names, why don't I take this opportunity to introduce myself . . . or I should say, my ACTUAL self, seeing as this is your final act as the 'Nameless Brat,'" Geri cackled to herself. "I am Geriatrix, and I am here to steal the youth from Oyster Cove's rather subpar middle school population!"

Geriatrix walked slowly around Emily in a grand display, fanning her arms in a royal flourish. She was clearly pleased as punch, and it made Emily want to reach out and scratch her face or mess up her hair, only she was still too stunned to move. She could not believe that her super-secret was out, and Amanda's, too!

"Maybe when your powers finally kick in, you'll be able to think of something *good* to call yourself," Geriatrix continued. "Or maybe I'll squash you both before that can ever happen, because I'll be hornswoggled if I'm going to let you diaper babies foil my plans."

Emily's face got hot. She looked around desperately for something to chuck at Geriatrix.

Geriatrix moved a water pitcher out of Emily's reach. "What, you think I didn't know about your boring little powers? Überhurling? Please. I've had my eyes on Oyster Cove for quite some time. I've been watching you, and I've influenced you to behave exactly as I wanted. I broke down your confidence and weakened your powers along the way—and then I got my sidekick—you may know him as Hoagie Joe—to lure you here. Trapping Bug Girl was easy . . . and trapping you will be even easier! And while you try oh-so-desperately to escape, I'll have my way at the dance. The wheels of my master plan are already turning. Once I drain the youth from not just a select few students but an entire middle school, I will stay young"— she started tallying up the years of youth to come on her fingers and then began laughing madly—"forever!" A couple of the white-haired women sitting close by startled. So did Emily, but she recovered quickly.

"You work with Hoagie Joe? Gross!" Emily blurted, forgetting the direness of her situation.

"Hoagie Joe has been my trusted employee for years," Geri said haughtily. "He gets jobs at schools as the cook. He watches you little monsters for a year or so, sizing up the population, so to speak, and lets me know when the time is ripe for me to 'transfer' in—when the student body's youth energy is at its peak. You rugrats never have any idea that the slop he cooks for you each day is filled with a special blend of herbs and spices designed to aid in my Y.E.T.—that stands for *Youth Energy Transfer*—so I can get the most bang for my buck."

"What's in it for him?" Emily asked. "I mean, he can't just enjoy forcing people to eat hot dog casserole."

Geri snorted. "I've promised to fulfill his lifelong dream," she said, her nose in the air, "and only I have the power to do it."

Emily laughed. "What's his dream—to learn how to

make a grilled cheese sandwich without burning it? He's the worst! You'd have a better accomplice if you were working with a bag of potting soil."

Geri scowled. "You're in no position to judge. Hoagie Joe may not be the freshest of fish, but he's loyal, and together we've got you right where I want you. When you get out—if you get out—it'll be too late for the students of Oyster Cove Middle School. Hoagie Joe and I will be long gone. He'll retire from a life of being a criminal accomplice, while I'll be off somewhere remote and exotic, being completely fabulous."

Geriatrix walked in increasingly smaller circles around Emily as she talked. Her skin really was flawless. It was like she didn't even have pores. "The 'ladies' of Disgruntled Pastures will continue playing cards and shuffling to their daily Jell-O-and-cottage-cheese luncheons, and there will be a whole school's worth of other oldsters to keep them company." Geriatrix patted Sadie Bimmins on the head. "And you and your creepy friend will have failed miserably at your second case. Failed! Because you are FAILURES! Oh, and PS . . .

"I'm still totally going to be Dancing Queen," the ancient crone said, batting her eyelashes. "But I'll think of you when I press the magic button on that disco ball remote."

Geriatrix booped Emily on the nose with her finger.

It was the last straw.

"Sit on it, grandma!" Emily shouted. "What are you even talking about? I'm not trapped. I'm standing right here, and I'm about to blast you back to the Stone Age, when you were born." Her face turned beet-red. Her entire body began to vibrate. She drew a deep breath through her clenched teeth and prepared to unleash the most piercing scream ever heard in the history of the entire universe.

But the moment Emily opened her mouth, Geriatrix calmly flipped a light switch beside the espresso contraption, and a huge box descended from the ceiling, dropping over Emily and sealing her inside.

Boom.

23

With bug powers come bug weaknesses, and Amanda had just discovered one of hers. She was caught in the clutches of a weird, hybrid couch-plant. The furniture's fragrance had lured her in just like a fly to a Venus flytrap, and now she was a goner! As the sofa's grip got tighter and tighter, the olfactory spell Amanda had fallen under began to fade. She squirmed to free herself, but it was too late—the couch just kept squeezing. As she struggled, the last packet of Cricket Crispies crunched in her pocket and fell onto the floor in a cloud of dust.

Outside of her own battle, Amanda could hear Emily slamming her fists against something and shouting. Her trapped partner was unleashing a slew of insults in Geria-trix's general direction, but the sinister senior wasn't pay-ing attention. She had turned her focus to Amanda.

"Save your strength, Bug Blunder. You'll never

escape my custom-grown sofa. It will consume you! And forget about your pathetic partner. She was poor competition in the popularity game, but she's an even worse hero."

Amanda managed to turn her head and stare directly at Geriatrix, her newly revealed enemy. Although she could feel the couch-plant's bright fibers digging into her skin like evil, acid-coated Velcro, she tried not to flinch or blink. She couldn't let Geriatrix know that she'd won.

"You may look young on the outside," Amanda said, "but your heart is black and bitter and tainted, and that will always show through your fake exterior. I could tell from the first moment I met you that you were no good. Selfish doesn't even begin to describe you! You're stealing people's lives! Why should YOU get an extended stay? You're the meanest, greediest person I've ever met, and that's saying a lot."

Geriatrix leaned in close to Amanda. "Oh, you're so sweet. Almost as sweet as the fragrance from my beautiful sofa. But your opinion of me is of little consequence.

Because in about twenty minutes, all of your friends will look like these old ladies at the card tables over here, and me? I'll be long gone, young and healthy forever. Forever! You failed before you'd even begun!"

A triumphant grin spread across Geriatrix's face. It was the same look that "Geri" got when handing out tickets.

"And another thing—you can shove your fashion tickets!" Amanda called after the villain as she sashayed out of the room.

Now Amanda was alone in her couch and Emily in her box. The old folks around them didn't even seem to notice.

"Emily!" Amanda shouted. Looking through a crack in the couch, Amanda could see her crime-busting partner in a panic, slamming her fists frantically against the walls of the box. She kicked, she punched, she flailed her fists, but even using her power punches and tremblor stomps, she was unable to make a dent in her cage. She crouched down, attempting to dig her fingers under the box's edge and overturn it. Amanda watched as Emily's face turned crimson. She struggled, straining to flip the container

over, but finally fell back, onto the floor. Growing desperate, she stood in the center of the cage and released one of her patented screams, but it reverberated around the walls and only succeeded in knocking her down. The poor girl looked . . . defeated.

"Emily, listen to me!" Amanda shouted, hoping her partner could hear her through the box's walls. "Emily, can you hear me?"

Emily stood and stumbled around, squinting at the walls.

"I can hear you, but I can't see you!" Emily finally responded. "I'm surrounded by mirrors." She squeezed her eyes shut and shook her head in dismay. "Boy, that creep Geriatrix sure got us good. I never suspected that she was THIS bad. This box she's got me trapped in weighs a ton. I can't get it to budge. Nothing I try will work! I'll be trapped here forever!"

It sure seemed like it.

But Amanda couldn't give up hope. Not yet. There was always a way out of dire situations; that was something Poppy had taught her early on in her training. "If you let hopelessness take control, you'll never get anywhere," he had said repeatedly. Poppy was usually right, and even though it was hard to see exactly how they were going to get out of this mess, there had to be a way. She just had to figure out what it was.

Luckily, Amanda had read all about Venus flytraps—in fact, she had even owned a few—and she knew from experience that once a bug got trapped in one of those things, it was next to impossible for it to get out. When the trigger hairs on the inside of the plant's trap were tripped, it would slam shut, capturing the bug inside. Having snared its prey, it would begin excreting digestive acids to slowly dissolve and eat the bug! That was what was happening to Amanda right now. If she didn't get out soon, she'd be this couch-plant-thing's dinner, but she knew that struggling would only make the trap squeeze tighter. So she tried to keep calm.

Emily wasn't following suit. She was acting up again, kicking and scratching and leaping around inside her box. She was wearing herself out.

"Emily, please!" Amanda cried. "Calm down. You're not helping anything! We need to be patient!"

"Calm down? Are you kidding? This is it. This is the end. All at the hands of that double-crossing . . . popularity thief!" Emily leaned against the side of her mirrored prison and slid down until she was slumped in a sitting position.

"Look, I know how you feel," Amanda shouted. And, boy, did she. "It's hard when you find out that your friend isn't really your friend."

"No. You don't know how I feel," Emily yelled back angrily. "Geri was never my friend, Amanda. I don't have friends! Not like you. I don't have friends, and I don't have wings, and I don't have a sidekick. I don't even have a supername!"

Amanda was speechless. It had never occurred to her that Emily was . . . jealous . . . of her! She tried to take a deep breath to help process this information, but the carnivorous couch was squeezing the bejesus out of her.

"That's not true," Amanda said as loudly as she could. "Everybody worships you. You have your own cool powers. And . . . I'm your friend."

Emily covered her face with her hands. She moved her fingers up into her hair until it looked like she might pull her pretty blond tresses right out. But then she slowly exhaled. "Well, that just makes me feel like more of a jerk," she sighed. "What if I'm just like her? What if I'm just like Geriatrix?"

If Amanda didn't know better, she'd swear that Emily was on the verge of tears.

Emily took a deep breath. "Look, Amanda, I need to tell you something in case we don't make it out of here. This won't be easy for me, because, well, I'm me, but I need to say it. I know I haven't been nice to you and that I'm the worst superhero partner in superhero history, but it's just that . . . everything comes so easily to you. And I'm failing. And I just . . . I've never felt this way before."

Amanda struggled with how to respond. Now she was not only paralyzed but speechless. On the one hand, she felt that Emily deserved to feel bad, because she most certainly HAD been the worst partner in superhero history . . . but Amanda didn't want to be petty. And she *did* want to escape.

"Emily, it's okay," she said. "When we get out of this, we will work it out, but right now—"

"Oh, I know I'm, like, the most popular person in the entire town, but that's different," Emily interrupted.

Amanda rolled her eyes. Even teetering on the brink of complete defeat, Emily's ego was unscathed.

"Having people want to *be* like you is not the same as having people *like* you," Emily continued. "Everyone I'm friends with just thinks they can get something from me. It's because of my social status, I guess. It's not the same as having real friends. You know—real friendships. Like the one I used to have with . . . well, you."

Amanda wondered if the couch toxins were dissolving her brain or affecting her hearing.

"Wait, what?" she blurted. "Are you for real right now? Do you know what you've put me through since we started middle school?"

"Amanda, I'm trying to say that I'm sorry, and that's a really big deal for me. I wasn't thinking about you. But I promise you this very instant that if we get out of here, I won't be all snotty toward you or any of your geeky friends ever again. It's not worth it. It makes me feel bad, you know, about myself." Emily paused for a second. "I'll even talk to you at school, in full view of other people."

"Excuse me, but could I get that in writing?" Amanda asked, half serious. She couldn't believe what she was hearing! "Because remember that you said something similar after we first teamed up, but it's been the cold shoulder or worse for me since school started."

"Look, I'll give it to you in writing, engraved on a

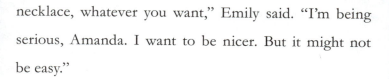

necklace, whatever you want," Emily said. "I'm being serious, Amanda. I want to be nicer. But it might not be easy."

Amanda smiled. That sounded like the truth. Although the couch was squeezing in on her harder than ever and she could barely breathe, she felt for the first time that she had a real partner.

And it was great.

VENUS FLYTRAP

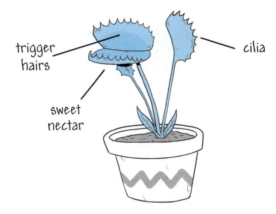

trigger hairs

cilia

sweet nectar

Fun Fact: The Venus flytrap attracts bugs by producing sweet nectar. Once its prey is close enough and hits the trigger hairs inside the plant's trap, the "mouth" snaps shut—and the plant eats the trapped insect!

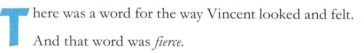

There was a word for the way Vincent looked and felt. And that word was *fierce*.

It should come as no surprise that Vincent took the Disco Daze theme of the dance seriously—after all, the 1970s were his second-favorite retro fashion era. Nor should it shock anyone who knew him that Vincent dazzled in a powder-blue polyester tuxedo with blue satin collar and trim, a blue ruffled shirt, and, of course, a blue satin bow tie. The ensemble was a homage to his grandfather's senior prom outfit. He'd seen it in old photos, and it was incredible, if he did say so himself.

The tux had been a real find. His mother had accompanied him to several vintage clothing stores around town in search of the perfect outfit. He'd finally discovered his dream ensemble at Lava Lamplighter's Vintage Couture. To top off the look, he was wearing old-school four-wheel roller skates with rainbow laces so he could boogie down to the hits of yesteryear in classic roller rink style.

Vincent set out for the dance in high spirits. He was fashionably late because of, you know, style. It took time to look this good. And a recent sidekick-training session had taught him the importance of being overprepared, so he had taken some extra time to pack for any possible surprises. "Always think ahead," Frida had drilled into him. "You need to carry things that you can't imagine you'll ever need." Vincent had scribbled down her every word in his Sidekick Journal.

"Grape jelly," Poppy had added when Frida was done. "You'll always need a good supply of grape jelly." Vincent hadn't questioned his trainer. No matter how strange the things that came out of Poppy's mouth sounded, they always turned out to be helpful.

Vincent was eternally

boogie-down smile!

groovy ruffles

satin collar

tuxedo in powder blue

retro roller skates

grateful to Frida and Poppy and their expanded knowledge. Sidekick training had boosted his confidence in totally unforeseen ways. For example, he no longer walked into a room waiting to be made fun of, and he didn't feel like he had to keep from saying exactly what he felt. He was stronger and happier, and he liked himself a whole lot more. Confidence of this magnitude was a new sensation—and it ruled.

As Vincent rolled up the sidewalk toward the gym, he noticed an abnormally large number of food trucks parked around the entrance. Sure, food trucks were all the rage, even in Oyster Cove, but wasn't a whole fleet overdoing it a bit? Especially considering that this was a middle school dance for students with an average allowance of five bucks

a week. Vincent counted at least ten rolling grease traps. The slippery, broken-down heaps featured names such as Croaky DeVane's Lacquered Turnip Chips; Meatballs of the World; Cubed Spam on a Stick; Aloysius McDrizzle's World-Famous Hot Dog Pockets; and perhaps most ominously, Earl Glubmuckle's WE FRY EVERYTHING Jamboree.

Gross. Vincent thought he'd pass.

He was doing the classic roller rink move where you squat down and hold one leg straight out in front of you, hovering over the sidewalk, when he spotted Hoagie Joe. He was hunched over, talking to . . . Geri!

"What the heck?" Vincent whispered. "What's Hoagie Joe doing talking to that meanie? He's the one who told us not to trust her! He ratted her out to us!"

Vincent rolled quietly around the Cubed Spam on a Stick truck to investigate. He came to a stop just out of Hoagie Joe's and Geri's eyesight, in a spot where he could hear every single nasty word they were saying.

"I captured them as easily as you said I would. And with Emily and Amanda out of the way, our plan will go through without a hitch," Geri boasted, chuckling to herself.

"This time, you'll be young forever," Hoagie Joe blathered. When he smiled, he looked even worse—if that was possible. "I had the new headbands made to your specifications! Once you hit that remote control and the disco ball starts spinning, the youthful zest will be drained right out of each and every one of these little creeps."

Geri gave the cook a stern look. "The final component of my plan has to happen right after that or it won't work," she hissed. "We need to make sure she's here."

"I'll do my part. You just see to it that I get the twenty-four-hour diner you promised me. I don't wanna keep messing around with these unappreciative brats," Hoagie Joe gurgled. "My dream of having a restaurant of my own, where I can serve my world-famous tuna puffs and oyster strudel, is finally within my reach, and I won't stand for any shenanigans, you got me?"

"You'll get your revolting restaurant," Geri said dismissively, "once the plan is complete."

Vincent couldn't listen to any more. His heart was

pounding, and he had to work hard to control his breathing. This was no time for an asthma attack! He needed to get to Amanda and Emily as fast as lightning. Thank goodness he was wearing his UltraZip 9000 skates! He rolled silently away from the two baddies and onto the road, picking up speed.

As he rolled past the Soft-Serve Cheeze Fries truck, he checked his spare tablet. His tracker app showed exactly where Geri had last been, and he expected that would be where he'd find Amanda and Emily. He just hoped he wasn't too late!

He followed the blinker, cruising toward the old abandoned Victorian-style home that previously housed Dr. Ronstein's Mad Hospital of the Doomed, zipping past the Craggy Swamp of Sorrow, and zooming around the bend by the Legendary Hideout of the Mortuary Twins. . . .

"Dang, where the heck is this tracker taking me?" Vincent wondered aloud as he whizzed past all the evil hotspots Oyster Cove had to offer. He had expected his search to end at any one of the many monuments paying respect to the town's troubled past—before Megawoman and Dragonfly had cleaned it up—but it did not.

When he finally turned onto Hibiscus Lane, he knew he was homing in on his target. But he couldn't believe what his target turned out to be.

"Disgruntled Pastures?" Vincent was perplexed. "This is a retirement home! What on earth would they be doing in here?"

But while his destination was odd, Vincent also knew that his tracking system was top-notch. After all, he himself had designed it.

He removed his skates, tiptoed up the building's steps, and went through its front doors. It was eerily devoid of personnel, a fact that troubled Vincent deeply. Seniors were prone to wander. He heard some movement behind a door labeled RECREATION ROOM and cautiously opened the door.

The first thing he saw was a group of women seated at card tables, enjoying what looked like peach yogurt.

"Pardon me, madames, but have you seen two young ladies about my age on the premises?" Vincent asked politely.

One of the women looked up at him. For a brief

moment, it seemed like she knew him. But then she turned back to her yogurt cup. The rest just stared blankly.

Something was off. Where were the attendants? Why were there no nurses? And what was that weird muffled sound?

Looking up, Vincent saw a scene that he could not believe he'd missed on his first glance. It was something akin to a horror movie, and in response, he squealed louder than he intended. On the far side of the large room, Amanda was smashed in what looked like a pair of giant, furry purple lips. Across from her, Emily was enclosed in a glass box and was pummeling the walls furiously with her fists.

"Amanda, what on earth?!" Vincent ran to his friend. Her face was bluish.

"It was Geri the whole time," Amanda managed to whisper. "She needs to be stopped. She's going to ruin everything."

"I know," Vincent said. "I snuck up on her talking to that fink Hoagie Joe outside the dance. They're planning something big! Remember what Synisteria told us? About not trusting anyone who offers advice in creepy situations? Boy, did she turn out to be right!"

"Vincent, you've got to get me out of here," Amanda gasped. "I can't breathe. Nothing I do works—Emily's tried all of her powers to escape, too. Even my bombardier beetle blast won't get through this thing!"

"I'll get you two out lickety-split," Vincent said— somewhat unconvincingly—as he looked around the room for anything to use as a tool. Finally, he raced over to the window and pulled the curtain rod off the wall.

Rushing back to Amanda, he jammed the metal rod in between the couch-plant's "lips." He used all his strength and full body weight to pry the thing open. Nothing. He hung off the rod like a fishing lure.

He hoped the box would be weaker.

Vincent ran out into the hall and soon flapped back in carrying a hammer he'd found in a utility closet. He pounded it against Emily's cage, but it didn't even make a scratch.

"What in the world is this thing made of?" Vincent wondered, baffled.

"Amanda, I don't know what to do," he finally blurted out, slumping down onto the floor next to the couch-plant. "I'm just not strong enough. And if we don't get out of here and back to the dance, Geri will suck the life out of the whole school! We don't have a moment to lose!"

"Not to mention the fact that this couch is eating me alive right now," Amanda squeaked. "There won't be much of me left if we can't figure a way to get me out of this thing!"

"Oh my," Vincent sighed, defeated. "My phone doesn't have a signal!"

"I refuse to give up," Amanda whispered, trying to sound more optimistic than she really was.

But as Vincent and Amanda racked their brains for a way out of their harrowing dilemma, a terrifying gurgling noise, like an underwater roar, echoed throughout the building. It was followed by the horrible sound of shattering glass and splintering wood.

Something was coming. Something big!

Amanda could barely turn her head to see what was stomping through Disgruntled Pastures, but from the sound of it, they were in the middle of another earthquake. Or maybe a typhoon. She craned her head just enough to see the door to the rec room splinter and burst apart.

In rippled an enormous, damp, froglike creature. The critter was about ten feet tall, with giant bulging eyes, and it was dripping goo all over the floor. It gurgled happily when it got all the way through the door.

"Rickie!" Vincent shrieked with glee. "OMG, I am so totally face-to-face with a real live cryptid!"

"CLETUS!" Amanda cried even louder, despite her predicament. She sounded as if she were being reunited with a long-lost friend, which, as a matter of fact, she was. Cletus, her sixth-grade science project in Mrs. Mallard's class, had lovably slithered back into her life. She had fond memories of growing him from a tadpole to a frog and then letting him go in the pond behind OCMS. And although he'd grown into this gigantic creature, Amanda would recognize his soulful eyes anywhere.

"Cletus? Are you sure?" Vincent stepped back, stunned, as the creature slogged over to the couch, leaving a trail of slime in his path.

"Yes, of course!" Amanda rasped. "He must have been transported to Rickets Lake from Cobbler's Pond via sewer runoff. . . . I bet the toxic gunk in Rickets caused him to mutate. And now he's an überamphibian!" Amanda was as animated as she could be while clamped inside a couch-plant's maw.

"Cletus!" she begged. "Get me out of here!"

The tadpole-turned-famous-lake-monster lumbered over to Amanda's couch-prison. With lightning speed, he shot his superfroggy tongue out and latched it to the upper lip of the couch. With a thundering stomp, he slapped one of his massive webbed feet onto the lower lip. With hardly any struggle at all, Cletus/Rickie pried that couch open, and Amanda unpeeled herself from its sticky innards.

Once Amanda was free, she gave the couch a swift kick. It squirmed a bit, heaved a sad sigh, and collapsed in a heap.

"Oh, Cletus!" Amanda cried, hugging the giant frog. "I'm so glad you're okay! But look what that lake did to you!"

"He looks fine to me," Vincent chimed in. "He's superstrong, and he just saved you. Speaking of which, can you get him to lift this cage off Emily before her head explodes? Although I have to admit, it's nice having her inside that box."

"Just because I can't see you doesn't mean I can't hear you," Emily shouted.

"All right, Cletus," Amanda said softly, "could you please get my friend out of there? Emily, do not freak out when you see Cletus! He is *nice*!"

Cletus lowered his head and slammed it into the side of Emily's cube. The rigid box must have weighed a ton because, in spite of his size, Cletus struggled against it. He tried a few times unsuccessfully before flapping his hind legs against the wall behind him. Using his legs like a giant jack, he pushed off against the wall.

That did it.

With a giant *thud*, the box toppled over, leaving Emily standing right in front of the giant frog creature. Her mouth fell open, and for once she was speechless.

"Emily, do you remember Cletus?" Amanda said, chuckling to herself. "He came to us from Rickets Lake to help."

"But how . . . ?" Emily stammered. "How did he know we were here?"

"I can only think it was the Cricket Crispies that fell out of my pocket while that creepy sofa was eating me," Amanda replied. "He must have a super sense of smell and been hungry for his favorite tasty snack!"

Emily nodded dumbly.

Cletus lumbered closer to Amanda and confirmed her

theory by slurping up the fallen Crispies—and their bag.

"Ladies," Vincent said, interrupting their reunion, "we have a definite situation at the dance that requires our immediate attention. You will both be happy to know that due to my foresight and also my sidekick training, I packed your hero outfits and have them here along with my own ensemble, which I might mention I have upgraded to look even more haute than it did before. It's pretty dang elegant, if I do say so myself."

Vincent tossed outfits to Amanda and Emily, who were super-ready for a change.

"Hey, Vincent, while we get into these outfits, can you turn off that espresso machine thing in the kitchenette? Geri, or Geriatrix, used it to drain the girls' essence and keep them docile!"

Vincent looked around the room and let Amanda's words sink in. "You mean these ladies? Oh!" He hustled over to the espresso machine as Amanda powered up.

In an instant Bug Girl stood in her place, exoskeleton glowing, wings unfurled, and ready to take flight. And Emily was, well, Emily in a costume. But they'd work on that part later. She was a shiny hero with great powers, even if she didn't have a name!

"Okay, Emily, let's go take Geriatrix down!" Bug Girl cried in a bid to boost Emily's morale.

Then Emily did something Bug Girl hadn't expected. She ran over and hugged her.

"I meant what I said," Emily insisted. "I'm going to do better. I promise. You know how I was totally jealous? I'm also really proud. I couldn't ask for a better partner."

"Okay, what's happening here?" Vincent asked, giving a little side-eye when he turned around and saw the two girls hugging.

"The future," replied Bug Girl, smiling.

"Well," Vincent warned, "in the present, we've got a fleet of food trucks blocking the exit to the dance, and a very sinister villain and her henchman passing out headbands to the unsuspecting students of Oyster Cove Middle School. Those headbands are going to do something really bad. . . . I just know it."

"We've got to get to the school before she drains the entire student body," Bug Girl commanded. "I won't allow that superficial creep to steal my classmates' childhoods!"

"And I've got a thing or two to say to her while we're at it," Emily added, slamming her left fist into her right hand and sending sparks flying. "She messed with the wrong tween queen."

"But, Vincent." Amanda paused. "Look at you!" Her friend had changed out of his vintage tuxedo and was standing before them in an extreme upgrade of his sidekick costume. Shimmering in green, with platform boots that came up to his knees, he looked every bit the superhero sidekick. His face was covered in what could only be described as eye-protecting high-tech glamour realness. "You look amazing!"

"You like it?" Vincent took a moment to show off. "Naturally, I designed it. Poppy helped with the manufacturing."

As the heroes were getting ready to take off, the girls whose essences had been drained began to shuffle toward them. With the zest machine disabled, they were already more mobile than they had been just an hour ago. And they wanted to go to the dance, too.

"Listen up," Bug Girl said to the assembled Oyster Cove elite. "You need to get to OCMS as quickly as possible. Call a cab or a bus, but just get there. And if we're lucky, we'll get you your youth back!"

"Yes, the dance," Sadie Bimmins wheezed, touching her cobweb-white hair. "We can't miss the dance!" With that, all of the OCMS students shuffled off to get ready.

"We'll see you there!" Bug Girl called after them. Emily, Vincent, and Cletus followed Bug Girl out of the damaged senior center and back down Hibiscus Lane toward the school.

Bug Girl took flight but kept pace with her grounded pals. Vincent, or Fanboy as he demanded to be called while in costume, pressed a button on his Fanboy boots to reveal embedded inline skates. As he raced down the road on his wheels, Emily ran beside him.

Cletus lagged behind. He wasn't as fast on land as he was in the water, and he was drying out. Bug Girl couldn't wait for her friend to catch up, though. There was too much at stake.

"Cletus, get back to Rickets Lake," Bug Girl called to

the giant amphibian. "I'll come see you as soon as all of this Geriatrix nastiness is resolved, I promise!" Bug Girl watched as the lake monster hopped off toward his polluted home. "And thanks!" she called.

As the heroes rounded the last bend toward OCMS, an eerie silence hovered in the air. The stench of fried foods and fattening desserts invaded Bug Girl's nose first and then she saw the trucks. "What is this, the Old West?" she called to her friends below.

The food trucks had created what looked like a wagon train around the entrance to the dance. No one could get out without passing through the barrier. In front of the food trucks, there were plenty of creepy-looking cooks standing around, ready to attack.

"Those goons in the hairnets must be Hoagie Joe's army," Bug Girl said as she fluttered down to the ground next to Emily and Fanboy. "We don't have time to fight them!"

"Let's sneak around the back," Fanboy suggested. "The trucks don't go all the way around the building!"

"Thank goodness Hoagie Joe isn't known for his brain," Emily quipped.

The three heroes took the long way around. Disco rhythms echoed from inside, and lights pulsed to the beat. Everything looked and sounded like a normal dance. At least from the exterior.

But as they approached the back entrance, they heard a scream so shrill, it made Bug Girl's blood run cold.

FROG

Fun Fact: A frog's sticky tongue is attached to the front of its mouth, unlike a human's tongue, which is attached at the back of the mouth. When it sees prey, a frog shoots its tongue out, catches its dinner, then swallows it down the back of its throat!

Frog tongues are so fast, they can catch food five times faster than a person can blink!

26

"**O**ver here!" Fanboy rolled up to the back entrance, held open the door, and waved everyone inside. Principal Pendelwort had neglected to station a chaperone beside the gymnasium's rear door, so all three of them ducked into the dance as quickly as they could and stood blinking in the disco lights.

The gym was transformed.

Light-up squares were pushed together to form a groovy dance floor in the center of the basketball court. Dazzling signs saying GET DOWN and BOOGIE OOGIE OOO-GIE! were hung over the bleachers. OCMS students were decked out in disco duds, and every one of them was wearing a glowing headband. To top it all off, the massive disco ball hung like a sequined moon from the peak of the ceiling right in the center of the room. It was not yet moving.

"Oh!" Fanboy gasped. The gymnasium was resplendent

with polyester. He had not seen so many bell-bottoms and platform shoes since his Uncle Chester's "Car Wash" party! But what made him gasp wasn't the abundance of overalls and other one-piece outfits (which always made bathroom visits such a challenge); it was something in the corner, something so horrifying that all he could do was point.

Emily turned to see what was upsetting the sidekick. Of course.

Geriatrix.

The villainess was dressed in a startlingly seventies maroon satin wrap dress that showed off her glowing necklace, and she had Cathy Swan backed into a corner behind the table of baked goods that Cathy had brought for refreshments. But cupcakes, cookies, muffins, pies, and doughnuts were not shield enough to protect her from Geriatrix's wrath.

Poor Cathy had her hands over her face. Emily wasn't sure if she was blocking the glow from the necklace or trying to hide the fact that she was crying.

Emily scanned the room. She wondered why Amanda's Bug Club wasn't helping Cathy. The science geeks usually flocked together. They usually helped one another out. *That's because they're friends*, Emily realized. But when she looked around, she saw all of the other kids dancing slowly—like they were in a daze. They were doing the bump and the bus stop and the hustle with absolutely zero style and rhythm. They were acting just like the youth-drained kids at Disgruntled Pastures!

"It's those headbands!" Emily yelled to Bug Girl and Fanboy. "Geri's sucking the life out of this party with those ugly headdresses. Get them off! Get them all off!"

The glowing circlets pulsed in rhythm with Geri's necklace and the relentless disco beat. Absolutely everyone was wearing one. Everyone except Cathy.

Fanboy reached out, only too happy to pluck off the offending bands, but he yanked his hand back quickly when he felt a jolt. The bands were electrified to prevent their removal.

In the corner of the gym, Geri was so intent on her bullying and so sure of her scheme that she didn't even notice that Bug Girl and Emily had busted out of her lousy traps and made it to the dance. She didn't even turn around when Emily got close. Instead she kept up her taunting, waving a headband in front of Cathy's face while the unpopular girl shivered.

"Go ahead and cry about it," Geri said, "but you have received too many fashion tickets to wear one of these. . . ." She dangled a headband over Cathy's head, waving it back and forth like it was a tasty treat. "I wouldn't give you one if you begged me . . . but go ahead. . . . Beg me."

"Geri, can't we just be friends?" Cathy near-whispered. "Please try one of these cayenne-mango-crème-filled doughnuts I created. It will lift your spirits. You'll see." Cathy placed the sugary treat on a pink napkin and offered it to the screeching bully.

Geri couldn't be bothered. "Thanks but no thanks. Being mean is much more fun than a sugar coma!" She took the doughnut from Cathy's trembling hand and dropped it on the floor.

Emily had seen enough. She stepped in between Cathy and Geri. For too long she'd turned a blind eye to Geri's cruel behavior. But no more. "Enough is enough! LEAVE

CATHY ALONE!" Emily shouted. "And dropping that doughnut was just rude!"

Geri was silenced for a nanosecond. A flicker of dissatisfaction crossed her face as she finally registered Emily's presence. Then her expression changed again to one of malevolent amusement.

"Who's going to stop me?" she asked, sneering at Emily. "*You?*"

"Yeah, *me*—" Emily started to respond, but words failed her as Geriatrix, without breaking eye contact, levitated off the floor. She floated in front of Emily, just high enough to look down on her. Her necklace pulsated, changing colors and glowing brighter. Her smile grew even crueler. She threw her hands into the air, like a fancy jazz dancer. Emily leaped back as electricity shot from Geri's fingers, cutting through the air like lightning.

Cathy screamed again. Emily gulped. Geriatrix wasn't just greedy and mean. She was supercharged!

"You heard what my partner said," Bug Girl yelled from across the gym. "You need to back off!"

Geriatrix whirled. Bug Girl whipped some bombardier

beetle blasts her way, but she waved them aside. While Geriatrix was occupied, Emily helped Cathy off the floor. Emily was shaken, but she'd had a moment with herself in that mirrored box. She'd stared herself in the eye and knew one thing for sure: What's right is right.

"I'm sorry that you've been treated so horribly, Cathy," Emily said. "But I think it's high time we fix a few things around here."

"You mean we should get even?" Cathy asked, her voice breaking.

"I mean we should get *mad*," Emily said. "Don't you feel like throwing something?"

"Yes!" Cathy nodded. "Yes, I do!" Cathy had all the ammunition she needed on her snack table. Emily, satisfied that Cathy would be okay for the moment, zipped over to a large basket of dodge balls. She wanted some ammunition that could pack a wallop. Her motions were a blur as she launched ball after ball at Geriatrix. Though Emily always found her mark, the humiliation spheres were not enough to interrupt the crackling bolts erupting from Geriatrix's fingertips.

Geriatrix blasted back. She pointed her charged fingers at Emily and let loose an electric stream. Emily was blown into the air, coming dangerously close to the disco ball. Luckily Bug Girl was able to catch her and bring her back down to the ground safely. Geriatrix discharged another round of crackling lightning; this time she almost torched one of Bug Girl's wings. But she missed. She seemed distracted, shooting looks at the snack and punch table. She was still focused on Cathy Swan, who was now popping up from behind the buffet to hurl cupcakes and slices of pie.

Splat. One of the cupcakes hit Geriatrix's cheek, frosting first. She let it slide off. Still hovering, she glided closer to the table. The look in her eyes was way beyond creepy.

"Stop picking on Cathy already!" Emily shouted.

Geriatrix didn't even turn to look at her.

"Keep her distracted," Bug Girl whispered in Emily's ear. "I'm going to try to release those plastic streamers so we can wrap this has-been up." She pointed at the shiny silver and gold decorations that had been hung across the ceiling in an attempt to make the gym look like a groovy club. The plastic was strong and hard to rip through, and Bug Girl bet that if they could wrap it around Geriatrix, she would be immobilized. But she had to act fast—the vindictive villain was about to float right underneath the streamers!

Emily ran to Cathy, who popped up to lob a pastry over Emily's head. It landed with a *splot* on Geriatrix's satin dress. The meanie shook it off.

"Seriously? Those are your best moves?" Emily shouted. "You're the worst Dancing Queen ever!"

While Emily tried to get a rise out of Geriatrix, Cathy spotted Bug Girl soaring overhead for the first time. She gasped and pointed. "Bug Girl!" Unfortunately, Cathy's delight drew attention to Bug Girl's plan.

Geriatrix also looked up and quickly understood what Bug Girl had in the works. She zapped the streamers with her electrified fingers. The sizzling, melting strands dropped onto the hero in a tangled heap, pinning her wings to her body. She plummeted toward the ground.

Geriatrix laughed.

Cathy covered her mouth in horror.

And Emily calmly stepped underneath Bug Girl's hurtling body. She caught her partner easily and lowered her gently to the ground.

"Thanks," Bug Girl said, stunned.

"Any time," Emily shot back. "That's what friends are for."

27

Bug Girl, tangled in a sticky mess and stunned by the new attitude of her partner, peered past the glistening streamers at the other OCMS students. Her fellow middle schoolers were still locked in a stupor doing the electric slide. She hoped no part of them was aware of the horror show their theme dance had become. But she didn't have much time to consider their mental health, because she and Emily were suddenly and violently blasted apart by a new round of charges issuing from Geriatrix's evil fingers.

The superduo was blown in opposite directions. Emily was slammed into the basketball scoreboard. Bug Girl careened across the blinking dance floor into the wrestling helmets, mats, and balls that were stored on the other side of the gym. The padded equipment avalanched down over her, burying her completely.

Flinging off scoreboard bits, Emily got to her feet and raced over to her partner. Her arms were a blur as she yanked away the stinky athletic gear. "Just hold your breath! I'll have you out in a flash!" she shouted.

She glanced Geriatrix's way to make sure she wasn't about to get zapped again. What she saw was worse. The sinister senior had turned her attention to poor Cathy Swan *again*. Cathy was all out of her custom baked goods and just stood there with frosting-covered fingers, shaking.

What is it with that jerk? Emily fumed. *Why can't she just leave Cathy alone?* She worked faster, tossing away sporting equipment so she could free Bug Girl and they could take care of business—together.

Mats flew and helmets bounced on the floor. Finally Emily saw one of Amanda's adorable feelers. It was a little crooked. She cleared away several basketballs, uncovering Bug Girl's head. She looked a bit smushed, and when she saw that Geri was harassing Cathy again, she blanched.

"I'm totally tied in volleyball net under here." Bug Girl motioned Emily away with her eyes. "You go. Save Cathy.

I'll worm my way out of this! Seriously, Cathy needs you."

Emily hated leaving her partner in such a state, but there was no time to argue. Geriatrix was cackling again, and that was always a bad sign.

The villainess scowled at Cathy. "I thought it would be enough to drain the vitality of only the socially acceptable students, but then I realized through the power of bullying that draining YOU is what will make my transformation permanent!" she jeered. "Once I've taken your youth, I will be young and evil forever!" Geriatrix let loose a malevolent cackle so defiantly sinister that the lights flickered.

Cathy cowered, trying to make herself as small as possible.

"I thought I told you to LEAVE CATHY ALONE!" Emily bellowed. The power of her voice blasted out the gymnasium's high windows. The bleachers shuddered, and the students doing the robot seemed momentarily shaken out of their catatonic states.

Geriatrix was unfazed. "Are you kidding, you pathetic 'popular' girl? You're just jealous because I stole all the attention away from you. Goes to prove how fleeting success and fame can be. You lost the dance and your followers all flocked to my side. Compared to me, you're nothing but a sad, empty shell in designer flats. And that's all you'll ever be. Sad. Empty. Boring. Pathetic. *Angry*. And now, if you'll excuse me . . ."

Geriatrix turned back to Cathy.

But she was wrong. Emily was so much more than "angry." Emily was madder than she had ever been. She was madder than she'd been in kindergarten when she hadn't won the milking competition because that prize always went to a boy. She was madder than she'd been when Frederick Blimpsfalt dumped finger paints on her designer-original smock in second grade. She was madder than she'd been in fifth grade when Mr. Goiterhosen told her to "smile" when she was in no mood to do anything of the sort.

The rage boiled up inside Emily like molten lava inside a volcano. She felt her skin grow warm, starting at her toes and moving up until it reached her cheeks. Her face flamed hotter than the sun. She was so mad that she was speechless, but the rage kept building until there was no place for it to go. She stared at Geriatrix, focusing every ounce of her outrage on the smug youth-sucker. She gave the horrible mean queen the stink eye so hard, you could almost smell it.

Then, without warning, two white-hot beams shot from Emily's eyes.

Around the edges of the room, the shuffling dancers threw their hands up to protect themselves from the intense light and heat. For Geriatrix, there was no protection. The beams pierced her like a thousand burning lasers, halting her attack. She dropped to the gym floor, clutching her middle and gasping.

"You're wrong, Geri. I'm not angry. I'm *furious*," Emily said while smoke curled around her head.

For a moment the only sound in the gym was Sister

Sledge's hit song "We Are Family." Then, from beneath the pile of athletic apparatus, Bug Girl's defiant fist appeared.

And that's when she gave her partner a name.

"Woo-hoo!" Bug Girl's shout echoed in the gym. "Go get her, *Fury*!"

28

"**F**ury. I absolutely love it!" Bug Girl's partner was elated by her new moniker. And Bug Girl felt relieved, too. Finally. A supername!

But there was no time to celebrate—they had work to do. Wriggling free of the tangle she was in, Bug Girl shoved off against the floor with all her might. She sent balls and nets flying as she soared into the air, ready for a fight, fists clenched and all powers at their peak performance levels. But what she saw took her breath away.

Most of the students were still under the glowing headbands' spell, grooving to get down around the gym. And they were all aging, just like the ladies at Disgruntled Pastures. Those headbands were working! She also saw Cathy still cowering. *At least she's safe for the moment*, Bug Girl thought.

Then Bug Girl saw what her partner was up to. Fury

was standing in place, staring at what looked like a campfire. Smoke rose from a lump in the middle of the dance floor. Then it twitched.

"Is that . . . ?" Bug Girl started to ask as she fluttered down for a landing next to her partner. Before Fury had a chance to answer, the clump stirred. Bug Girl watched in horror as the pile shook itself off and, with great effort, stood up.

Coughing and wheezing, the entity before them brushed away the smoldering ash and looked at her arms disapprovingly before lifting her head and letting out a wail so terrifying that Bug Girl almost started crying.

"Geriatrix?" Bug Girl finally managed to squeak out. What had once been a popular student at Oyster Cove Middle School had now aged beyond belief. Long, wiry white hair cascaded from her head like piles of Spanish moss. The skin covering her bony arms and face resembled scrambled eggs pebbled with warts and moles. Her fingers were long spindles tipped with yellowed talons. The bags under her sunken eyes were charcoal gray. She wasn't old. She was ancient. And she was really, really angry.

"I blasted her," Fury boasted. "I shot these totally cool flashes right out of my eyes!" Fury put her hands on her hips. "Turns out I'm totally amazing after all, and you called it!"

Bug Girl was glad her partner had her confidence back. She sensed that they were about to need all the strength they could muster. Geriatrix was shuffling toward them!

"Oh, you little jerks!" Geriatrix seethed. "Just look what you've done to me, after I worked so hard and for so long! I'm showing my *age*!"

"Cheating nature never ends well," Bug Girl said. "Aging is something we all have to go through. It looks to me like you're just getting what you deserve for stealing youth for so long. Your outside now matches your inside—nasty, shriveled, and mean."

Geriatrix did not enjoy Bug Girl's lecture. With a wave of

her hand, she shot flashes of energy out of her fingertips that sent Bug Girl and Fury flying across the gym. And she wasn't done.

"Hoagie Joe!" Geriatrix screamed so loudly that it drowned out the music.

With a crash, the gym's doors burst open. Hoagie Joe, still covered in unidentifiable lipids and sauce, stomped over to the grizzled fiend and stood at attention. It took great effort, but Geriatrix managed to claw herself up onto Hoagie Joe's back and latch her arms around his neck.

"Get the Food Truck Army in here, and make sure Cathy Swan doesn't escape!" she ordered. "Those meddling kids might have temporarily aged me, but I still hold the key to immortality."

The hulking chef pulled a bullhorn out from the nether reaches of his slimy apron and blasted it three times. "You little creeps are in for it now," Hoagie Joe bleated at Bug Girl and Fury as Geriatrix chuckled maniacally over his shoulder. "I never liked cooking for you chumps, anyway. Ungrateful—that's what you are. Do you know how hard it is to come up with innovative creations to satisfy an entire school's cravings and meet the federal nutrition standards? All I ever hear from you is 'This is gross!' or 'I want grilled cheese!' Well, forget you!"

Hoagie Joe ended his rant just as what sounded like a stampede echoed into the gym. All the chefs and workers that had been tending to the food trucks rushed into the middle of the dance.

"I knew there was more to those food trucks than met the eye!" Bug Girl whispered to her partner. "Get ready, Fury! This is where your irritation is totally going to come in handy."

Bug Girl saw that Fanboy was still trying to get head-bands off of students' heads with no success. And the students were aging more with each passing second.

"Fanboy!" Bug Girl called to her sidekick. "Stay with Cathy and keep her safe! We'll figure out the headbands after this battle is over!"

"Yes, ma'am," Fanboy replied, trotting over to where Cathy was hiding.

Bug Girl knew Cathy was in good hands. Not only was Fanboy super-duper smart, he was also the best sidekick a hero could ever hope for. She took a millisecond to reflect on how lucky she was to have him before refocusing on the fight before her. The food truck villains stood at attention with pots, pans, tongs, and other food-themed weapons ready for action.

"Get 'em!" Hoagie Joe hollered as Geriatrix, still on his back, flailed her hands in the air.

Earl Glubmuckle of deep-frying fame was the first to strike. He floundered toward the two heroes with what looked like a cookie press. When he fired it, a spray of grease shot out and got all over Fury's silver unitard.

Time seemed to stand still.

Bug Girl sucked in a deep, deep breath as Fury looked down at the mess on her costume. Some of the grease had dribbled onto her boots.

"Oh no," Fury said almost calmly. Too calmly. "Oh no, you did NOT just get grease on my getup." She tapped her foot. She turned slowly to Bug Girl, who was gearing up to retaliate. "Oh, I've got this one," she said, turning the corner of her mouth up into a half smile. Her hands balled into fists. She planted her feet firmly. She looked directly into Earl Glubmuckle's eyes. Then she lifted her left foot and slammed it down with such force that Earl went flying right up into the rafters. He managed to grab on to a beam and cling there for dear life.

"One down," Fury said with satisfaction. "All right, Bug Girl, let's get this over with so we can disco dance to at least one song."

Bug Girl nodded and high-fived her partner. "You take the left, I'll take the right. We'll meet in the middle. That's where Geriatrix and that double agent Hoagie Joe are going down!"

Bug Girl turned to a chef who was rushing at her. He whipped bologna slices like throwing stars. They stuck to her carapace and slowed her down until she shot some well-placed bombardier beetle blasts on them. The boiling chemical compound disintegrated the gross sandwich fixings instantly. She ran right at the lunchmeat-flinging fiend and flipped him over, knocking him unconscious.

She plowed through a few more culinary cretins with ease, thwarting Pastrami Pete with her soundwave-blasting tymbals, the Cupcake Priestess with a mean praying mantis punch, and tripping Ernesto the Bratwurst King as he ran toward her, whipping a link of sausages around like a nunchaku.

"Gross," she said to him as the links flew right out of his hands.

One by one, all of the food truck creeps on Bug Girl's side of the gym fell to her superpowers. Cooks and sous-chefs slumped over in smelly, food-stained piles surrounded by oblivious dancers still under the spell of their glowing headbands.

Bug Girl knew they had to get those bands off before they did permanent damage! She turned just in time to see Fury jump up and stuff the Gyro Master directly into a basketball hoop, where he was left dangling and flailing his arms. Fury had taken out each and every food truck baddie on her side of the gym. One turkey—Davey Drumstick—had recovered slightly and was trying to make a run for it, but Fury picked up a dodge ball and blasted him in the back of the head with it.

"Point," Bug Girl hooted.

The partners stood back-to-back with their hands on

their hips; it had been a satisfying showdown. But their revelry was short-lived.

Bug Girl and Fury heard Fanboy's muffled cry at the same time. They whirled around to see Hoagie Joe towering over the sidekick, threatening him with an eggbeater. Apparently Hoagie Joe had summoned Pizza Pammy to help hold Fanboy, who was squirming and kicking but not getting anywhere thanks to a web of stringy cheese and slime. "You leave her alone," the skinny boy shouted, unconcerned about his own safety. His eyes were locked on a terrifying scene behind the overturned table.

Geriatrix had shimmied down from Hoagie Joe's back. The prune-like criminal had backed Cathy into a corner and was holding a new, elaborate headband, covered in what looked like jewels and mirrors, over her head.

"You wanted this," Geriatrix cackled. "Now hold still while I give it to you!" She started to lower the dreadful youth-draining tiara.

Cathy was frozen—petrified with fear.

Bug Girl and Fury launched themselves at their aged adversary, desperate to stop her from sucking the life out of sweet Cathy Swan, but as they got close, Geriatrix whipped her head around and pointed a gnarled finger at them.

"One step closer and I'll drop this headband on Cathy's head," Geriatrix screeched. "And you will have saved NO ONE."

"You're planning to drop that headband on her anyway, so cut the drama, lady," Fury retorted.

The hero partners glanced at each other knowingly and then Fury shouted again, "Hey, Cathy, how do you get your frosting so light and fluffy?"

"Whip it!" Cathy screamed. And she began to pummel Geriatrix with her fists. Her balled-up hands moved so fast, they were a blur. She knocked the tainted headband away and continued with the beatdown. Fury was seriously impressed.

Geriatrix curled into a ball, covering her head with her arms, and Cathy darted out from behind the table to stand with the heroes. Fury fist-bumped the baker while Bug Girl launched herself into the air.

She buzzed past Geriatrix, diving close to the gym

floor to snatch the final headband from the vile villain's reach. She crumpled the device into a small ball and flung it across the gym, where it clanged against the far wall.

"No!" Geriatrix cried, but it was too late. Her plan had been foiled.

Bug Girl turned and aimed her next attack at Hoagie Joe and Pizza Pammy.

"Do NOT mess with my sidekick," she yelled.

Pizza Pammy ran away, leaving a trail of sauce.

"Hey!" Hoagie Joe shouted after her. "You're one lousy accomplice!"

"So much for your stupid army," Fury yelled at Hoagie Joe as Fanboy squeezed out from under the gross cheese strands. "Oh, and by the way, your food stinks. I mean, how many disgusting ways are there to desecrate hot dogs? Your techniques are amateur and your recipes flawed."

Landing next to Fury, Bug Girl saw Hoagie Joe sniffle. Clearly Fury had touched a nerve.

"I think I'm a good cook," he whimpered. His shoulders shook.

"Shut up, all of you!" Geriatrix demanded. "You think

you're so great," she hissed, pointing at Fury and Bug Girl. "I came in and took over this school. I get away with everything because I am eternal! And I will prevail again! You two are defeated!"

Geriatrix raised her claws and let go of what should have been a blast of energy. It sparked and fizzled, leaving her fingers limp and singed.

"No! NO! I won't be old! I won't!" she screeched.

"I think you will," Fury countered. She rushed forward and snatched the glowing necklace from Geriatrix's withered throat. "In fact you already are!"

"Give that back! Give it to me!" Geriatrix demanded, scrambling toward her former Dancing Queen rival. "That is mine and I need it!"

"Personally, I think this thing is outdated," Fury said sarcastically, holding it out of the villain's reach. "You need to live in the now."

Without the necklace, the last bit of Geriatrix's power drained from her body. She slumped down onto the floor next to Hoagie Joe, who was sobbing over Fury's food-related insults.

"It's tacky, too," Fanboy said judgmentally. "May I?"

Fanboy took the necklace from Fury, holding it far from his body, between his thumb and index finger. Then, using the remote control, he lowered the disco ball to the floor and attached the necklace to it. With another push, he sent the ball back up to its rightful place above the dance floor.

"While I was unsuccessful at getting students to remove those ghastly headbands, I did formulate a way to reverse the effects," Fanboy said. "At least, I hope I did."

Fanboy handed the disco ball remote to Fury. "Hit it, Dancing Queen."

Fury backed away from the rest of the group. "I've dreamed about this my whole life," she said, her eyes welling up. "But I never could have gotten here without you guys."

"Come on, come on," Fanboy said. "This isn't the Academy Awards."

"No, seriously," Fury said.

Bug Girl rolled her eyes, but she was grinning. "Just give us a break and press the button."

Fury grinned back. Then the Dancing Queen held the remote over her head, pressed the button, and shouted loud enough to be heard in three counties: "Let's dance!"

Everyone—Bug Girl, Fury, Fanboy, Geriatrix, and Hoagie Joe—craned their heads toward the ceiling as the mirrored ball slowly began its hypnotic spin.

As the ball turned faster and the lights reflected off of its mirrored surfaces, it sent starlight around the gymnasium. Its sparkling reflections were magical.

And they were working. Geriatrix's necklace glowed brighter and brighter as the lights reflected off the ball. Finally, the necklace shone so brightly that it became difficult to look at. Beams shot out of it and were reflected off the disco ball's faceted surface, raining down onto the dancing students below and zapping them. One by one, as they were hit by the beams, the students regained their youth and their minds. They looked around the gym with dazed expressions, wondering exactly how long the dance had been going on.

Fanboy dashed from student to student and snatched the powerless (and tacky) headbands off of each muzzy head.

The ladies of Disgruntled Pastures shuffled into the gym just in time to catch the regenerative beams raining down from the altered disco ball. Once restored, they too skipped into the center of the gym and danced to the hits of yesteryear, as if nothing out of the ordinary had happened at all.

Bug Girl, Fury, and Fanboy rushed over to the refreshment table to check on Cathy Swan. She was dancing! Carefree and spinning to the beat, she waved to her new friends.

"I feel amazing!" she called. "This is so much fun!"

A gargling noise at the gymnasium's entrance let Bug Girl know that Cletus had come back to make sure she was safe. She flew over to her friend and put her hands on his bumpy, smiling face.

"Thank you for your help," Bug Girl said to the giant frog. "You will always be my friend." Fury and Fanboy joined her.

"Here," Cathy Swan cooed, running over. She handed Cletus a specialty cake. "I didn't put this on the table because, well, it's made of mealworms. I was hoping I'd get to give it to you!"

Cletus took the treat and croaked his appreciation.

"What is that *thing*?" Geriatrix sputtered from across the room. "It's hideous!"

"Look in a mirror, sister," Fury shouted. "This is Rickie, and he is amazing!"

Bug Girl could see that Cletus needed to get back to the water. His skin was drying out again. "You'd better go," she warned her friend. "We want you to stay around for a long time."

The former cryptid and current local celebrity hopped away as Bug Girl and her friends watched.

"Come on!" Cathy waved as she ran back to the middle of the gym.

The heroes all joined her in one quick dance before getting back to work.

"Let's lock up that louse Geriatrix and her creepy cook sidekick," Fury shouted to Bug Girl over the music.

"With pleasure, partner." Bug Girl smiled.

29

"**I**t sounds like you had quite an adventure," Amanda's mom said. She and Megawoman had finally returned from their out-of-town conference only to discover that their daughters had thwarted yet another villainous plot in Oyster Cove.

"I'll say it was," Amanda replied. She was looking at the front page of the local paper. The headline read BUG GIRL AND FURY OUST GERIATRIC BADDIE AND CHEF SIDEKICK. As soon as all the reporters hovering around Rickets Lake had heard the commotion over at OCMS, they'd high-tailed it over just in time to witness the final moments of the battle. A photographer had even captured Bug Girl and Fury dragging Geriatrix and Hoagie Joe off to jail!

"And they did it as actual partners, by gum," Poppy added, flinging some oatmeal across the table as he excitedly waved his spoon. "Finally, those two girls came to their senses!"

Amanda couldn't help smiling. She was so relieved that Emily had not only become a true hero but had apologized for everything also. She had her best friend back. She was about to say as much when the doorbell rang.

When Amanda went to answer it, she found Emily, Mrs. Battfield, and Frida.

"Hi!" Emily said. "Ready to go to school?" She pushed her way past Amanda and walked toward the kitchen. Amanda and the others followed.

"We just came to escort our heroes to class," Mrs. Battfield said. "We're so proud of what proactive, strong young women you are!"

"And now starts your most important training," Frida

BUG GIRL AND FURY OUST GERIATRIC
BADDIE AND CHEF SIDEKICK

added. "Poppy and I are taking you to Hero Level 2.0 starting this week!"

Amanda got nervous. She couldn't imagine what other level there might be. . . . She'd toppled sinister villains and saved the town more than once. "Don't we even get a week off?" she blurted. "We just saved the entire school!"

"You must always be vigilant, always training," Frida said. "For you never know what new evil will rear its ugly face in our little town!"

"You're darn tootin'," Poppy added. "Why, in your mother's day we'd start training again as soon as she'd dragged a baddie off to the clink. No time for lying around feeling proud when there's ne'er-do-wells on the loose." He spooned a canned peach into his mouth.

"Ugh, enough already." Emily walked toward the door. "Come on, Amanda! We'll be late."

Everything at Oyster Cove Middle School was about as normal as it could be, given the circumstances. Amanda noted that all of the students were back, healthy and pretty much the same. Sadie Bimmins and Lorricent Grandy stared openmouthed when Amanda and Emily walked past them together.

"I guess I can expect some of that," Emily whispered to Amanda. "But I can handle them, and if they get out of line, I'll take care of it. There will be no more bullying here if I can help it."

Amanda and Emily rounded the corner just in time to see the Entomological Society gathering at their lockers. Sh'Shelle looked wary as they approached, but Amanda gave her a reassuring look to let her know that Emily meant no harm.

"Hi, guys, what's going on?" Amanda said to the group.

"We were just going over today's Rickets Lake Bioremediation Roundup," Vincent said. "The vats are a great success, and the water is clearing up nicely. The city is offering to dredge up all of the refuse that's been dumped there over the years. They want to make Rickets a biological preserve and make Rickie the official Oyster Cove mascot!"

"You mean Cletus," Amanda corrected her friend. "He is a very special amphibian."

"I'm going over there after school to visit with him," Cathy Swan said. "He needs friends, and I love watching him swim and jump. I baked him a cake using cricket flour. It stinks, but I bet he'll love it."

Amanda was relieved that Cathy was getting more involved and allowing her personality to shine through.

"Hey, Cathy, would you mind if I come with you?" Emily asked. "I mean, I guess I should, like, thank Rickie for helping Bug Girl and Fury save the dance or something."

Amanda and all of her friends went completely silent. Lars Viddlehammer dropped his books. Arnix Detricklium almost fainted.

"Well, sure, I think that would be nice," Cathy finally offered. "I'll meet you after school. We could even walk there if you want."

"Let's all go." Emily smiled. "It'll be fun!"

EPILOGUE

Weeks passed, and all over Oyster Cove leaves began to turn strange and wondrous colors. Temperatures dropped, sweaters came out of storage, and the nights were laced with a chill. The fireflies had blinked their last twilight flashings for the year, and pumpkins piled up on doorsteps.

After an extraordinarily short trial (there was zero doubt about their guilt, especially when Geriatrix shouted, "And I'd do it all again! I'll get even with each and every one of you if it's the last thing I do!"), Geriatrix and Hoagie Joe had been locked up in prison. A new chef—with blander sensibilities when it came to cafeteria food—was hired. And a sense of calm was established at OCMS.

The new ordinary was wonderful. No name-calling, no tripping in the halls, nothing. And to top it off, Emily was even hanging out with Amanda and her friends on a regular basis. She LIKED working on the Rickets Lake Bioremediation Roundup. Emily liked science!

On everyone's mind at the moment, however, was the upcoming Oyster Cove Middle School Halloween Pageant and Bake-Off. Every year the school held a massive carnival. All the teachers and students dressed up and were encouraged to enter their baked goods in the competition. "No anchovies," the competition's rules finally stated the year after the Hovelhopper family had sent each of its seven children to school with anchovy cupcakes for nine years running.

Amanda was walking down the hall with Emily, talking about what to bake, when she noticed something amiss.

"Would you care to purchase a chocolate bar?" Tiffany Spigots practically screamed. "You need to buy one of these bars. It's for a good cause!"

"What's it for?" Amanda asked. She wasn't going to just give money to any old thing. She had principles.

"It's for the civics club," Tiffany replied. And then, in a near-robotic voice, she continued, "For we are raising moneys with which to take a group tour of our nation's capital at a date to be determined in the future."

"Sounds like a scheme to me," Emily interrupted. "Beat it."

Amanda peered down the hall. "Emily, look."

Tiffany wasn't the only sugar pusher. Up and down the locker bank, students were being harassed to buy chocolate. By other students.

"It's for the civics club" was the explanation each seller

gave as they thrust chocolate bars in people's faces. "Buy one. Buy it now."

"Since when do we even have a civics club?" Emily shouted down the hall. "I mean, who wants to talk about civics in their off-time? Boring."

"You must buy this chocolate," yet another kid blathered. Amanda noticed his eyes were not looking at her but past her. At nothing at all. He was creepy. "Buy this chocolate."

"No thank you," Amanda responded, her concealed antennae fluttering. Oh, great. She thought of a creamy and delicious bowl of fettuccine al fredo as she and Emily pushed past the candy peddler and into class.

She took her seat toward the front of the room. Vincent came in and sat next to her.

"I got this great chocolate," he said, gnawing on a hunk. "Would you care for a piece?"

"Vincent, put that down," Amanda said. "There's something wrong with it, mark my words!"

"But it's delicious, and don't you want to help the civics club?"

"No, I most certainly do not. Now put that candy down!" She knew Poppy had told Vincent to listen to her when it came to matters like this. "And pay attention. Here comes Mr. Schenkenclabber."

Vincent tried to sneak a final bite, but Emily forcefully smacked the bar out of his hands and onto the floor with a look that made him whimper.

As the teacher entered, all chattering ceased. Today they were supposed to be doing litmus-paper experiments, something Amanda had been looking forward to all year. She loved watching the special paper change colors depending on what it touched. She had bottles of litmus paper stored up in anticipation of this very lecture and lab project.

"Students," Mr. Schenkenclabber droned after taking attendance, "today I have a very important assignment. Each of you is to take a box of this chocolate and sell it to your friends, family, neighbors, and anyone you can stop long enough to talk to, for we are raising moneys with which to send our venerated civics club on a tour of our nation's capital at a date to be determined in the future."

Amanda couldn't believe it. She turned to Emily. Her partner nodded.

They had work to do. And it started with civics.

ACKNOWLEDGMENTS

With a new book we got a new editor, and what an editor we got in Mr. John Morgan. Sir, your twenty-page treatise on *Bug Girl 2* was insightful, humorous, helpful, and made clear that you love Oyster Cove and its denizens as much as we do. Thank you for shepherding them, and us, through the process. We'd also like to thank Erin Stein for the chance to tell the further tales of Amanda and Emily, Ellen Duda for her amazing design, the marketing and production teams at Imprint, and, of course, Anoosha Syed for her superb and adorable illustrations.

B.H. & S.H.S.

I would like to thank Sarah. She is a fabulous writing partner and an even more fabulous friend—and superfun to work with. A very large thank-you goes to Mr. Isaac Prado for being a wonderful and supportive treehugger and my best friend. He changed my life. And of course, I'd like to thank my parents. Among other reasons, a chunk of this book would be way different if it weren't for them allowing me to watch Dr. Paul Bearer's cheesy horror movie double features on local TV when I was a child. I'd also like to thank Rachel Barry, who gave me lots of great advice throughout this process. Finally, I'd like to thank everyone who takes the little extra bit of time needed to move a bug (or spider) out of the way. They thank you, too!

B.H.

I've got gobs of gratitude for Ben, the bug whisperer, who makes me laugh and never ceases to surprise me. It is a pleasure to write with you. I'm also extremely grateful to my husband, Nathan, who brings me coffee EVERY morning. I could not do a dang thing without him, or coffee. Okay, I might be exaggerating. I could probably do things, but I wouldn't want to. I'd like to thank my kids for keeping me in check and remembering to empty the dishwasher and take out the trash. More thanks go to the rest of my family, my bookstore families, and my incomparable friends who have been wonderfully supportive of Bug Girl, and me. Also, thank you for not littering.

S.H.S.

ABOUT THE AUTHORS

Sarah Hines Stephens grew up in the foothills of the Sierra Nevada mountains, where she liked to build habitats for woolly bear caterpillars and roller-skate in the carport. She has been a bookseller, an editor, a ghostwriter, an author, a garden instructor, and a lab assistant—and still holds many of those jobs. She makes her home in Oakland, California, where she lives with three humans, two dogs, and an ever-changing cast of house spiders.

Benjamin Harper is originally from St. Petersburg, Florida, where hot summers fostered his love of bugs. After going to school in western North Carolina, he moved to New York City to pursue a career in publishing. He has been involved in children's books as both an editor and author for almost as long as he can remember. Currently, he lives in Los Angeles, California, where he raises monarch butterflies and lives with a cat, a dog, and a hippie.

About the Illustrator

Anoosha Syed is a freelance illustrator and concept artist for animation. She is a graduate of Ceruleum Ecole d'arts Visuels in Switzerland and is currently living in Toronto. Select clients include Lacoste, Walmart, Simon & Schuster, and Nickelodeon. Her work has also been featured on BuzzFeed and Nerdist. When Anoosha isn't drawing for work, she's drawing for fun. (She doesn't really have any other hobbies.)